THE GOOD HUSBAND OF ZEBRA DRIVE

Much is happening on Zebra Drive and Tlokweng Road. Precious Ramotswe is experiencing staffing difficulties. First, Mr J.L.B. Matekoni asks to be put in charge of a case involving an errant husband. But can a man investigate such matters as successfully as the number one lady detective can? Then, Mma Ramotswe has a falling out with her assistant Mma Makutsi, who decides to leave the agency, taking her near-perfect secretarial skills with her.

Along the way, Mma Ramotswe is asked to investigate a couple of tricky cases. Will she be able to explain an unexpected series of deaths at the hospital in Mochundi? And what about the missing office supplies at a local printing company? These are the types of question that Mma Ramotswe is uniquely well suited to answer.

In the end, whatever happens, she knows she can count on Mr J.L.B. Matekoni, who stands for all that is solid and true in a shifting world, and there is always her love of Botswana, a country of which she is justifiably proud.

THE GOOD HUSBAND OF ZEBRA DRIVE

Alexander McCall Smith

WINDSOR
PARAGON

First published 2007
by
Polygon, an imprint of Birlinn Ltd
This Large Print edition published 2007
by
BBC Audiobooks Ltd by arrangement with
Birlinn Ltd

Hardcover ISBN: 978 1 405 61770 3
Softcover   ISBN: 978 1 405 61771 0

British Library Cataloguing in Publication Data available

Printed and bound in Great Britain by
Antony Rowe Ltd., Chippenham, Wiltshire

This book is for

Tom and Sheila Tlou

THE GOOD HUSBAND
OF ZEBRA DRIVE

CHAPTER ONE

A Very Rude Person

It is useful, people generally agree, for a wife to wake up before her husband. Mma Ramotswe always rose from her bed an hour or so before Mr J.L.B. Matekoni—a good thing for a wife to do because it affords time to accomplish at least some of the day's tasks. But it is also a good thing for those wives whose husbands are inclined to be irritable first thing in the morning—and by all accounts there are many of them, rather too many, in fact. If the wives of such men are up and about first, the husbands can be left to be ill-tempered by themselves—not that Mr J.L.B. Matekoni was ever like that; on the contrary, he was the most good-natured and gracious of men, rarely raising his voice, except occasionally when dealing with his two incorrigible apprentices at Tlokweng Road Speedy Motors. And anybody, no matter how even-tempered he might be, would have been inclined to raise his voice with such feckless young men. This had been demonstrated by Mma Makutsi, who tended to shout at the apprentices for very little reason, even when one of them made a simple request, such as asking the time of day.

'You don't have to shout at me like that,' complained Charlie, the older of the two. 'All I asked was what time it was. That was all. And you shout *four o'clock* like that. Do you think I'm deaf?'

Mma Makutsi stood her ground. 'It's because I

know you so well,' she retorted. 'When you ask the time it's because you can't wait to stop working. You want me to say five o'clock, don't you? And then you would drop everything and rush off to see some girl or other, wouldn't you? Don't look so injured. I know what you do.'

Mma Ramotswe thought of this encounter as she hauled herself out of bed and stretched. Glancing behind her, she saw the inert form of her husband under the blankets, his head half covered by the pillow, which was how he liked to sleep, as if to block out the world and its noise. She smiled. Mr J.L.B. Matekoni had a tendency to talk in his sleep—not complete sentences, as one of Mma Ramotswe's cousins had done when she was young, but odd words and expressions, clues each of them to the dream he was having at the time. Just after she had woken up and while she was still lying there watching the light grow behind the curtains, he had muttered something about brake drums. So that was what he dreamed about, she thought—such were the dreams of a mechanic; dreams of brakes and clutches and spark plugs. Most wives fondly hoped that their husbands dreamed about them, but they did not. Men dreamed about cars, it would seem.

Mma Ramotswe shivered. There were those who imagined that Botswana was always warm, but they had never experienced the winter months there—those months when the sun seemed to have business elsewhere and shone only weakly on southern Africa. They were just coming to the end of winter now, and there were signs of the return of warmth, but the mornings and the evenings could still be bitterly cold, as this particular

2

morning was. Cold air, great invisible clouds of it, would sweep up from the south-east, from the distant Drakensberg Mountains and from the southern oceans beyond; air that seemed to love rolling over the wide spaces of Botswana, cold air under a high sun.

Once in the kitchen, with a blanket wrapped about her waist, Mma Ramotswe switched on Radio Botswana in time for the opening chorus of the national anthem and the recording of cattle bells with which the radio started the day. This was a constant in her life, something that she remembered from her childhood, listening to the radio from her sleeping mat while the woman who looked after her started the fire that would cook breakfast for Precious and her father, Obed Ramotswe. It was one of the cherished things of her childhood, that memory, as was the mental picture that she had of Mochudi as it then was, of the view from the National School up on the hill; of the paths that wound through the bush this way and that but which had a destination known only to the small, scurrying animals that used them. These were things that would stay with her forever, she thought, and which would always be there, no matter how bustling and thriving Gaborone might become. This was the soul of her country; somewhere there, in that land of red earth, of green acacia, of cattle bells, was the soul of her country.

She put a kettle on the stove and looked out of the window. In mid-winter it would barely be light at seven; now, at the tail end of the cold season, even if the weather could still conjure up chilly mornings like this one, at least there was a little more light. The sky in the east had brightened and the first rays of the sun were beginning to touch the tops of the trees in her yard. A small sun bird—Mma Ramotswe was convinced it was the same one who was always there—darted from a branch of the mopipi tree near the front gate and descended on the stem of a flowering aloe. A lizard, torpid from the cold, struggled wearily up the side of a small rock, searching for the warmth that would enable him to start his day. Just like us, thought Mma Ramotswe.

Once the kettle boiled, she brewed herself a pot of red bush tea and mug in hand went out into the garden. She drew the cold air into her lungs and when she breathed out again her breath hung in the air for a moment in a thin white cloud, quickly gone. The air had a touch of wood smoke in it from somebody's fire, perhaps that of the elderly watchman at the nearby government offices. He kept a brazier fire going, not much more than a few embers, but enough for him to warm his hands on in the cold watches of the night. Mma Ramotswe sometimes spoke to him when he came off duty and began to walk home past her gate. He had a place of sorts over at Old Naledi, she knew, and she imagined him sleeping through the day under a hot tin roof. It was not much of a job, and he would have been paid very little for it, so she had occasionally slipped him a twenty-pula note as a gift. But at least it was a job, and he had a place to lay his head, which was more than some people had.

She walked round the side of the house to inspect the strip of ground where Mr J.L.B. Matekoni would be planting his beans later in the

4

year. She had noticed him working in the garden over the last few days, scraping the soil into ridges where he would plant, constructing the ramshackle structure of poles and string up which the bean stalks would be trained. Everything was dry now, in spite of one or two unexpected winter showers that had laid the dust, but it would be very different if the rains were good. If the rains were good . . .

She sipped at her tea and made her way to the back of the house. There was nothing to see there, just a couple of empty barrels that Mr J.L.B. Matekoni had brought back from the garage for some yet-to-be-explained purpose. He was given to clutter, and the barrels would be tolerated only for a few weeks before Mma Ramotswe would quietly arrange for their departure. The elderly watchman, Mr Nthata, was useful for that; he was only too willing to take away things that Mr J.L.B. Matekoni left lying about in the yard; Mr J.L.B. Matekoni forgot about these things fairly quickly and rarely noticed that they had gone.

It was the same with his trousers. Mma Ramotswe kept a general watch on the generously cut khaki trousers that her husband wore underneath his work overalls, and eventually, when the trouser legs became scuffed at the bottom, she would discreetly remove them from the washing machine after a final wash and pass them on to the woman at the Anglican Cathedral who would find a good home for them. Mr J.L.B. Matekoni often did not notice that he was putting on a new pair of trousers, particularly if Mma Ramotswe distracted him with some item of news or gossip while he was in the process of getting dressed. This was necessary, she felt, as he had always been unwilling

5

to get rid of his old clothes to which, like many men, he became excessively attached. If men were left to their own devices, Mma Ramotswe believed, they would go about in rags. Her own father had refused to abandon his hat, even when it became so old that the brim was barely attached to the crown. She remembered itching to replace it with one of those smart new hats that she had seen on the top shelf of the Small Upright General Dealer in Mochudi, but had realised that her father would never give up the old one, which had become a talisman, a totem. And they had buried that hat with him, placing it lovingly in the rough board coffin in which he had been lowered into the ground of the land that he had loved so much and of which he had always been so proud. That was long ago, and now she was standing here, a married woman, the owner of a business, a woman of some status in the community; standing here at the back of her house with a mug that was now drained of tea and a day of responsibilities ahead of her.

She went inside. The two foster children, Puso and Motholeli, were good at getting themselves up and did so without any prompting by Mma Ramotswe. Motholeli was already in the kitchen, sitting at the table in her wheelchair, her breakfast of a thick slice of bread and jam on a plate before her. In the background, she could hear the sound of Puso slamming the door of the bathroom.

'He cannot shut doors quietly,' said Motholeli, putting her hands to her ears.

'He is a boy,' said Mma Ramotswe. 'That is how boys behave.'

'Then I am glad that I am not a boy,' said

6

Motholeli.

Mma Ramotswe smiled. 'Men and boys think that we would like to be them,' she said. 'I don't think they know how pleased we are to be women.'

Motholeli thought about this. 'Would you like to be somebody else, Mma? Is there anybody else you would like to be?'

Mma Ramotswe considered this for a moment. It was the sort of question that she always found rather difficult to answer—just as she found it impossible to reply when people asked when one would like to have lived if one did not live in the present. That question was particularly perplexing. Some said that they would have liked to live before the colonial era, before Europe came and carved Africa up; that, they said, would have been a good time, when Africa ran its own affairs, without humiliation. Yes, it was true that Europe had devoured Africa like a hungry man at a feast—and an uninvited one too—but not everything had been perfect before that. What if one had lived next door to the Zulus, with their fierce militarism? What if one were a weak person in the house of the strong? The Batswana had always been a peaceful people, but one could not say that about everybody. And what about medicines and hospitals? Would one have wanted to live in a time when a little scratch could turn septic and end one's life? Or in the days before dental anaesthetic? Mma Ramotswe thought not, and yet the pace of life was so much more human then and people made do with so much less. Perhaps it would have been good to live then, when one did not have to worry about money, because money did not exist; or when one did not have to fret

7

about being on time for anything, because clocks were as yet unknown. There was something to be said for that; there was something to be said for a time when all one had to worry about was the cattle and the crops.

And as for the question of who else she would rather be, that was perhaps as unanswerable. Her assistant, Mma Makutsi? What would it be like to be a woman from Bobonong, the wearer of a pair of large round glasses, a graduate—with ninety-seven per cent—of the Botswana Secretarial College, an assistant detective? Would Mma Ramotswe exchange her early forties for Mma Makutsi's early thirties? Would she exchange her marriage to Mr J.L.B. Matekoni for Mma Makutsi's engagement to Phuti Radiphuti, proprietor of the Double Comfort Furniture Store—and of a considerable herd of cattle? No, she thought she would not. Manifold as Phuti Radiphuti's merits might be, they could not possibly match those of Mr J.L.B. Matekoni, and even if it was good to be in one's early thirties there were compensations to being in one's early forties. These were ... She stopped. What precisely were they?

Motholeli, the cause of this train of thought, now interrupted it; there was to be no enumeration of the consolations of being forty-ish. 'Well, Mma,' she said. 'Who would you be? The Minister of Health?'

The Minister, the wife of that great man, Professor Thomas Tlou, had recently visited Motholeli's school to present prizes and had delivered a stirring address to the pupils. Motholeli had been particularly impressed and had talked

8

about it at home.

'She is a very fine person,' said Mma Ramotswe. 'And she wears very beautiful headdresses. I would not mind being Sheila Tlou ... if I had to be somebody else. But I am quite happy, really, being Mma Ramotswe, you know. There is nothing wrong with that, is there?' She paused. 'And you're happy being yourself, aren't you?'

She asked the question without thinking, and immediately regretted it. There were reasons why Motholeli would prefer to be somebody else; it was so obvious, and Mma Ramotswe, flustered, searched for something to say that would change the subject. She looked at her watch. 'Oh, the time. It's getting late, Motholeli. We cannot stand here talking about all sorts of things, much as I'd like to ...'

Motholeli licked the remnants of jam off her fingers. She looked up at Mma Ramotswe. 'Yes, I'm happy. I'm very happy. And I don't think that I would like to be anybody else. Not really.'

Mma Ramotswe sighed with relief. 'Good. Then I think ...'

'Except maybe you,' Motholeli continued. 'I would like to be you, Mma Ramotswe.'

Mma Ramotswe laughed. 'I'm not sure if you would always enjoy that. There are times when I would like to be somebody else myself.'

'Or Mr J.L.B. Matekoni,' Motholeli said. 'I would like to know as much about cars as he does. That would be good.'

And dream about brake drums and gears? wondered Mma Ramotswe. And have to deal with those apprentices, and be covered in grease and oil half the time?

Once the children had set off for school, Mma Ramotswe and Mr J.L.B. Matekoni found themselves alone in the kitchen. The children always made a noise; now there was an almost unnatural quiet, as at the end of a thunderstorm or a night of high winds. It was a time for the two adults to finish their tea in companionable silence, or perhaps to exchange a few words about what the day ahead held. Then, once the breakfast plates had been cleared up and the porridge pot scrubbed and put away, they would make their separate ways to work, Mr J.L.B. Matekoni in his green truck and Mma Ramotswe in her tiny white van. Their destination was the same—the No. 1 Ladies' Detective Agency shared premises with Tlokweng Road Speedy Motors—but they invariably arrived at different times. Mr J.L.B. Matekoni liked to drive directly to the top of the Tlokweng Road along the route that went past the flats at the end of the university, while Mma Ramotswe, who had a soft spot for the area of town known as the Village, would meander along Oodi Drive or Hippopotamus Road and approach the Tlokweng Road from that direction.

As they sat at the kitchen table that morning, Mr J.L.B. Matekoni suddenly looked up from his teacup and started to stare at a point on the ceiling. Mma Ramotswe knew that this preceded a disclosure; Mr J.L.B. Matekoni looked at the ceiling when something needed to be said. She said nothing, waiting for him to speak.

'There's something I meant to mention to you,'

he said casually. 'I forgot to tell you about it yesterday. You were in Molepolole, you see.'

She nodded. 'Yes, I went to Molepolole.'

His eyes were still fixed on the ceiling. 'And Molepolole? How was Molepolole?'

She smiled. 'You know what Molepolole is like. It gets a bit bigger, but not much else has changed. Not really.'

'I'm not sure that I would want Molepolole to change too much,' he said.

She waited for him to continue. Something important was definitely about to emerge, but with Mr J.L.B. Matekoni these things could take time.

'Somebody came to see you at the office yesterday,' he said. 'When Mma Makutsi was out.'

This surprised Mma Ramotswe and, in spite of her equable temperament, irritated her. Mma Makutsi had been meant to be in the office throughout the previous day, in case a client should call. Where had she been?

'So Mma Makutsi was out?' she said. 'Did she say where?' It was possible that some urgent matter of business had arisen and this had required Mma Makutsi's presence elsewhere, but she doubted that. A more likely explanation, thought Mma Ramotswe, was urgent shopping, probably for shoes.

Mr J.L.B. Matekoni lowered his gaze from the ceiling and fixed it on Mma Ramotswe. He knew that his wife was a generous employer, but he did not want to get Mma Makutsi into trouble if she had deliberately disobeyed instructions. And she had been shopping; when she had returned, just before five in the afternoon—a strictly token return, he thought at the time—she had been

11

laden with parcels and had unpacked one of these to show him the shoes it contained. They were very fashionable shoes, she had assured him, but in Mr J.L.B. Matekoni's view they had been barely recognisable as footwear, so slender and insubstantial had seemed the criss-crossings of red leather which made up the upper part of the shoes.

'So she went shopping,' said Mma Ramotswe, tight-lipped.

'Perhaps,' said Mr J.L.B. Matekoni. He tended to be defensive about Mma Makutsi, whom he admired greatly. He knew what it was like to come from nowhere, with nothing, or next to nothing, and make a success of one's life. She had done that with her ninety-seven per cent and her part-time typing school, and now, of course, with her well-heeled fiancé. He would defend her. 'But there was nothing going on. I'm sure she had done all her work.'

'But something did turn up,' pointed out Mma Ramotswe. 'A client came to see me. You've just said that.'

Mr J.L.B. Matekoni fiddled with a button on the front of his shirt. He was clearly embarrassed about something. 'Well, I suppose so. But I was there to deal with things. I spoke to this person.'

'And?' asked Mma Ramotswe.

Mr J.L.B. Matekoni hesitated. 'I was able to deal with the situation,' he said. 'And I have written it all down to show you.' He reached into a pocket and took out a folded sheet of paper, which he handed to Mma Ramotswe.

She unfolded the paper and read the pencil-written note. Mr J.L.B. Matekoni's handwriting was angular, and careful—the script of one who

12

had been taught penmanship, as he had been, at school all those years ago, a skill he had never forgotten. Mma Ramotswe's own handwriting was less legible and was becoming worse. It was something to do with her wrists, she thought, which had become chubbier over the years and which affected the angle of the hand on the paper. Mma Makutsi had suggested that her employer's handwriting was becoming increasingly like shorthand and that it might eventually become indistinguishable from the system of pencilled dashes and wiggles that covered the pages of her own notebook.

'It will be a first,' she remarked, as she squinted at a note which Mma Ramotswe had left her. 'It will be the first time that anybody has started to write shorthand without learning it. It may even be in the papers.'

Mma Ramotswe had wondered whether she should feel offended by this, but had decided to laugh instead. 'Would I get ninety-seven per cent for it?' she asked.

Mma Makutsi became serious. She did not like her result at the Botswana Secretarial College to be taken lightly. 'No,' she said. 'I was only joking about shorthand. You would have to work very hard at the Botswana Secretarial College to get a result like that. Very hard.' She gave Mma Ramotswe a look which implied that such a result would be well beyond her.

Now, on the paper before her, were Mr J.L.B. Matekoni's notes. 'Time,' he had written, '3.20 p.m. Client: woman. Name: Faith Botumile. Complaint: husband having an affair. Request: find out who the husband's girlfriend is. Action

13

proposed: get rid of girlfriend. Get husband back.'

Mma Ramotswe read the note and looked at her husband. She was trying to imagine the encounter between Faith Botumile and Mr J.L.B. Matekoni. Had the interview taken place in the garage, while his head was buried in some car's engine compartment? Or had he taken her into the office and interviewed her from the desk, wiping his hands free of grease as she told her story? And what was Mma Botumile like? What age? Dress? There were so many things that a woman would notice which would provide vital background to the handling of the case which a man simply would not see.

'This woman,' she asked, holding up the note. 'Tell me about her?'

Mr J.L.B. Matekoni shrugged. 'Just an ordinary woman,' he said. 'Nothing special about her.'

Mma Ramotswe smiled. It was as she had imagined, and Mma Botumile would have to be interviewed again from scratch.

'Just a woman?' she mused.

'That's right,' he said.

'And you can't tell me anything more about her?' asked Mma Ramotswe. 'Nothing about her age? Nothing about her appearance?'

Mr J.L.B. Matekoni seemed surprised. 'Do you want me to?'

'It could be useful.'

'Thirty-eight,' said Mr J.L.B. Matekoni.

Mma Ramotswe raised an eyebrow. 'She told you that?'

'Not directly. No. But I was able to work that out. She said that she was the sister of the man who runs that shoe shop near the supermarket.

14

She said that she was the joint owner, with him. She said that he was her older brother—by two years. I know that man. I know that he had a fortieth birthday recently because one of the people who brings in his car for servicing said that he was going to his party. So I knew . . .'

Mma Ramotswe's eyes widened. 'And what else do you know about her?'

Mr J.L.B. Matekoni looked up at the ceiling again. 'Nothing, really,' he said. 'Except maybe that she is a diabetic.'

Mma Ramotswe was silent.

'I offered her a biscuit,' said Mr J.L.B. Matekoni. 'You know those iced ones you have on your desk. In that tin marked *Pencils*. I offered her one of those and she looked at her watch and then shook her head. I have seen diabetics do that. They sometimes look at their watch because they have to know how long it is before their next meal.' He paused. 'I am not sure, of course. I just thought that.'

Mma Ramotswe nodded, and glanced at her own watch. It was almost time to go to the office. It was, she felt, going to be an unusual day. Any day on which one's suppositions are so rudely shattered before eight o'clock is bound to be an unusual day, a day for discovering things about the world which are quite different from what you thought they were.

She drove into work slowly, not even trying to keep up with Mr J.L.B. Matekoni's green truck ahead of her. At the top of Zebra Drive she nosed her van out across the road that led north, narrowly avoiding a large car which swerved and sounded its horn; such rudeness, she thought, and

15

so unnecessary. She drove on, past the entrance to the Sun Hotel and beyond it, against the hotel fence, the place where the women sat with their crocheted bedspreads and table-cloths hung out for passers-by to see and, they hoped, to buy. The work was intricate and skilfully done; stitch after stitch, loop after loop, worked slowly and painstakingly out from the core in wide circles of white thread, like spider-webs; the work of women who sat there so patiently under the sun, women of the sort whose work was often forgotten or ignored in its anonymity, but artists really, and providers. Mma Ramotswe needed a new bedspread and would stop to buy one before too long; but not today, when she had things on her mind. Mma Botumile. Mma Botumile. The name had been tantalising her, because she thought that she had encountered it before and could not recall where. Now she remembered. Somebody had once said to her: *Mma Botumile: rudest woman in the whole of Botswana. True!*

CHAPTER TWO

The Rule of Three

'So, Mma,' said Mma Makutsi from behind her desk. 'Another day.'

It was not an observation that called for an immediate reply; certainly one could hardly contradict it. So Mma Ramotswe merely nodded, glancing at Mma Makutsi and taking in the bright red dress—a dress which she had not seen before.

16

It was very fetching, she thought, even if a bit too formal for their modest office; after all, new clothes, grand clothes, can show just how shabby one's filing cabinets are. When she had first come to work for Mma Ramotswe, Mma Makutsi had possessed only a few dresses, two of which were blue and the others of a faded colour between green and yellow. With the success of her part-time typing school for men, she had been able to afford rather more, and now, following her engagement to Phuti Radiphuti, her wardrobe had expanded even further.

'Your dress, Mma,' said Mma Ramotswe. 'It's very smart. That colour suits you well. You are a person who can wear red. I have always thought that.'

Mma Makutsi beamed with pleasure. She was not used to compliments on her appearance; that difficult skin, those too-large glasses—these made such remarks only too rare. 'Thank you, Mma,' she said. 'I am very pleased with it.' She paused. 'You could wear red too, you know.'

Mma Ramotswe thought: *of course I can wear red.* But she did not say this, and simply said, instead, 'Thank you, Mma.'

There was a silence. Mma Ramotswe was wondering where the money for the dress came from, and whether it had been bought during that unauthorised absence from work. She thought that she might know the answer to the first question: Phuti Radiphuti was obviously giving Mma Makutsi money, which was quite proper, as he was her fiancé, and that was part of the point of having a fiancé. And as for the second question, well, she would be able to find that out readily enough.

17

Mma Ramotswe strongly believed that the simplest way to obtain information was to ask directly. This technique had stood her in good stead in the course of countless enquiries. People were usually willing to tell you things if asked, and many people moreover were prepared to do so even if unasked.

'I always find it so hard to make up my mind when I'm choosing clothes,' said Mma Ramotswe. 'That's why Saturday is such a good time for clothes-shopping. You have the time then, don't you? Unlike a working day. There's never time for much shopping on a work day, don't you find, Mma Makutsi?'

If Mma Makutsi hesitated, it was only for a moment. Then she said, 'No, there isn't. That's why I sometimes think that it would be nice not to have to work. Then you could go to the shops whenever you wanted.'

Silence again descended on the office. For Mma Ramotswe, the meaning of Mma Makutsi's comment was quite clear. It had occurred to her before now that her assistant's engagement to a wealthy man might mean her departure from the agency, but she had quickly put the idea out of her mind; it was a possibility so painful, so unwelcome, that it simply did not bear thinking about. Mma Makutsi might have her little ways, but her value as a friend and colleague was inestimable. Mma Ramotswe could not imagine what it would be like to sit alone in her office, drinking solitary cups of bush tea, unable to discuss the foibles of clients with a trusted confidante, unable to share ideas about difficult cases, unable to exchange a smile over the doings of the apprentices. Now she felt ashamed of herself in having begrudged Mma

18

Makutsi her shopping trip during working hours. What did it matter if a conscientious employee slipped out of the office from time to time? Mma Ramotswe herself had done that on numerous occasions, and had never felt guilty about it. Of course, she was the owner of the business and had nobody to account to apart from herself, but that fact alone did not justify having one rule for herself and one for Mma Makutsi.

Mma Ramotswe cleared her throat. 'Of course, one might always take a few hours off in the afternoon. There's nothing wrong with that. Nothing at all. One cannot work all the time, you know.'

Mma Makutsi was listening. If she had intended her remark to be a warning, then it had been well heeded. 'Actually, I did just that the other day, Mma,' she said casually. 'I knew that you wouldn't mind.'

Mma Ramotswe was quick to agree. 'Of course not. Of course not, Mma.'

Mma Makutsi smiled. This was the response she had hoped for, but Mma Ramotswe could not be let off that easily. 'Thank you.' She looked out of the window for a moment before continuing, 'Mind you, it must be a very nice, free feeling not to work at all.'

'Do you really think so, Mma?' asked Mma Ramotswe. 'Don't you think you'd become bored rather quickly? Particularly if you left a job like this, which is such an interesting one. I would miss it very badly, I'm afraid.'

Mma Makutsi appeared to give the matter some thought. 'Maybe,' she said, non-committedly. And then added, as if to emphasise the doubtfulness of

Mma Ramotswe's proposition, 'Perhaps.'

The matter was left at that. Mma Makutsi had made her point—that she was now a woman who did not actually need the job she occupied, and who would go shopping if she wished; and for her part, Mma Ramotswe had been made to understand that there had been a subtle shift in power, like a change in the wind, barely noticeable, but nonetheless there. She had always been a considerate employer, but her seniority in age, and in the business, had lent her a certain authority that Mma Makutsi had always recognised. Now that things appeared to be changing, she wondered if it would be Mma Makutsi, rather than herself, who decided when tea break was to be. And would it stop at that? There was always Mr Polopetsi to be considered. He was the exceedingly mild man to whom Mma Ramotswe had given a job—of sorts—after she had knocked him off his bicycle and had heard of his misfortunes. He had proved to be a keen worker, capable of helping Mr J.L.B. Matekoni in the garage as well as taking on small tasks for the agency. He was both unobtrusive and eager to please, but she had already heard Mma Makutsi referring to him as 'my assistant' in a tone of voice that was distinctly proprietorial, even though there had never been any question but that she was herself an assistant detective. Mma Ramotswe wondered whether Mma Makutsi might now claim to be something more than that, a *co-detective*, perhaps, or better still an *associate detective*; there were many ways in which people could inflate the importance of their jobs by small changes to their titles. Mma Ramotswe had met an associate professor from the university, a man who brought his car to Mr J.L.B. Matekoni for repair. She had reflected on his title, imagining that this would be appropriate for one who was allowed to associate with professors, without actually being allowed to be one himself. And when they had tea, these professors, did the associate professors drink their tea while sitting at the edge of the circle, or a few yards away perhaps—of the group but not quite of it? She had smiled at the thought; how silly people were with their little distinctions, but here she was herself thinking of some way of bringing Mma Makutsi forward, but not too far forward. That, of course, would be a way of keeping her assistant. It would be easy enough to give her a nominal promotion, particularly if no salary increase was required. This would be an exercise in window-dressing, in tokenism; but no, she would do this because Mma Makutsi actually deserved it. If she was to become an associate detective, with all that that implied—whatever that was—it would be because she had earned the title.

'Mma Makutsi,' she began. 'I think that it is time to have a review. All this talk of jobs and not working and such matters has made me realise that we need to review things . . .'

She got no further. Mma Makutsi, who had been looking out of the window again, had seen a car draw up to park under the acacia tree.

'A client,' she said.

'Then please make tea,' said Mma Ramotswe.

As Mma Makutsi rose to her feet to comply, Mma Ramotswe breathed a discreet sigh of relief. Her authority, it seemed, was intact.

*   *   *

21

'So, we're cousins!' said Mma Ramotswe, her voice halfway between enthusiasm and caution. One had to be careful about cousins, who had a habit of turning up in times of difficulty—for them—and reminding you of cousinship. And the old Botswana morality, of which Mma Ramotswe was a stout defender, required that one should help a relative in need, even if the connection was a distant one. There was nothing wrong with that, thought Mma Ramotswe, but at times it could be abused. It all depended, it seemed, on the cousin.

She glanced discreetly at the man sitting in the chair in front of her desk, the man whom Mma Makutsi had spotted arriving and whom she had ushered into the office. He was well dressed, in a suit and tie, and his shoe laces, she noticed, were carefully tied. That was a sign of self-respect, and such evidence, together with his open demeanour and confident articulation, made it clear that this was not a distant cousin on the scrounge. Mma Ramotswe relaxed. Even if a favour was about to be asked for, it would not be one which would require money. That was something of a relief, given that the income of the agency over the past month had been so low. For a moment she allowed herself to think that this might even be a paying case, that the fact that the client was a cousin would make no difference when it came to the bill. But that, she realised, was unlikely. One could not charge cousins.

The man smiled at her. 'Yes, Mma. We are cousins. Distant ones, of course, but still cousins.'

Mma Ramotswe made a welcoming gesture with her hands. 'It is very good to meet a new cousin.

But I was wondering . . .'

'How we are related?' the man interrupted. 'I can tell you that quite simply, Mma. Your father was the late Obed Ramotswe, was he not?'

Mma Ramotswe nodded in confirmation: Obed Ramotswe—her beloved Daddy—the man who had raised her after the death of the mother she could not remember; Obed Ramotswe, the man who had scrimped and saved during all those hard, dark years down the mines and who had built up a herd of cattle that any man might be proud of. Not a day went past, not a day, but that she thought of him.

'He was a very fine man, I have been told,' said the visitor. 'I met him once when I was much younger, but we had left Mochudi, you see, and we were living down in Lobatse. That is why we did not meet, you and I, even though we are cousins.'

Mma Ramotswe encouraged him to continue. She had decided that she liked this man, and she felt slightly guilty about her initial suspicions. You had to be careful, some people said; you had to be, because that was how the world had become, or so such people argued. They said that you could no longer trust people, because you did not know where other people came from, who their people were; and if you did not know that, then how could you trust them? Mma Ramotswe saw what was meant by such pronouncements, but did not agree with this cynical view. Everybody came from somewhere; everybody had their people. It was just a bit harder to find out about them these days; that was all. And that was no reason for abandoning trust.

Their visitor took a deep breath. 'Your late

23

father was the son of Boamogetswe Ramotswe, was he not? That was your grandfather, also late?'

'That was.' She had never known him, and there were no pictures of him, as was usually the case with people of that generation. Nobody knew any more how they looked, how they dressed. All that was lost now.

'And he had a sister whose name I cannot remember,' the man went on. 'She married a man called Gotweng Dintwa, who worked on the railways back in the Protectorate days. He was in charge of a water tower for the steam trains.'

'I remember those towers,' said Mma Ramotswe. 'They had those long canvas pipes hanging down from them, like an elephant's trunk.'

The man laughed. 'That is what they were like.' He leaned forward. 'He had a daughter who married a man called Monyena. He was your father's generation and they knew one another, not very well, but they knew one another. And then this Monyena went to Johannesburg and was thrown in jail for not having the right papers. He came back home to his wife and settled near Mochudi. That is where I come in. I am that man's son. I am called Tati Monyena.'

He uttered the last sentence with an air of pride, as a storyteller might do at the end of a saga when the true identity of the hero is at last revealed. Mma Ramotswe, digesting the information, allowed her gaze to move off her guest and out of the window. There was nothing happening outside the window, but you never knew. The acacia tree might be still, its thorny branches unmoved by any breeze, with just the pale blue sky behind them, but birds landed there and watched, and moved,

24

and led their lives. She thought of what had been told her—this potted story of a family that had shared roots with her own. A few words could sum up a lifetime; a few more could deal with a sweep of generations, whole dynasties, with here and there a little detail—a water tower, for instance— that made everything so human, so immediate. It was a distant link indeed, and she was as closely connected to him as she was to hundreds, possibly thousands of other people. Ultimately, in a country like Botswana, with its sparse population, everybody was connected in one way or another with virtually everybody else. Somewhere in the tangled genealogical webs there would be a place for everybody; nobody was without people.

Mma Makutsi, who had been listening from her desk, now decided to speak. 'There are many cousins,' she said.

Tati Monyena turned round and looked at her in surprise. 'Yes,' he said. 'There are many cousins.'

'I have so many cousins,' Mma Makutsi continued. 'I cannot count the number of cousins I have. Up in Bobonong. Cousins, cousins, cousins.'

'That is good, Mma,' said Tati Monyena.

Mma Makutsi snorted. 'Sometimes, Rra. Sometimes it is good. But I see many of these cousins only when they want something. You know how it is.'

At this, Tati Monyena stiffened in his chair. 'Not everybody sees their cousin for that reason,' he muttered. 'I am not one of those who . . .'

Mma Ramotswe threw a glance at her assistant. She might be engaged to Phuti Radiphuti now, but she had no right to speak to a client like that. She would have to talk to her about it, gently, of course, but she would have to remonstrate with her.

'You are very welcome, Rra,' Mma Ramotswe said hurriedly. 'I am glad you came to see me.'

Tati Monyena looked at Mma Ramotswe. There was gratitude in his eyes. 'I haven't come to ask a favour, Mma,' he said. 'I mean to pay for your services.'

Mma Ramotswe tried to hide her surprise, but failed, as Tati Monyena felt constrained to reassure her once more. 'I shall pay, Mma. It is not for me, you see, it's for the hospital.'

'Don't worry, Rra,' she said. 'But what hospital is this?'

'Mochudi, Mma.'

That triggered so many memories: the old Dutch Reformed Mission Hospital in Mochudi, now a government hospital, near the meeting place, the kgotla; the hospital where so many people she knew had been born, and had died; the broad eaves of which had witnessed so much human suffering, and kindness in the face of suffering. She thought of it with fondness, and now turned to Tati Monyena and said, 'The hospital, Rra? Why the hospital?'

His look of pride returned. 'That is where I work, Mma. I am not quite the hospital administrator, but I am almost.'

The words came quickly to Mma Ramotswe. 'Associate administrator?'

'Exactly,' said Tati Monyena. The description clearly pleased him, and he savoured it for a few moments before continuing, 'You know the hospital, Mma, don't you? Of course you do.'

Mma Ramotswe thought of the last time she had

been there, but put that memory out of her mind. So many had died of that terrible disease before the drugs came and stopped the misery in its tracks, or did so for many; too late, though, for her friend of childhood, whom she had visited in the hospital on that hot day. She had felt so powerless then, faced with the shadowy figure on the bed, but a nurse had told her that holding a hand, just holding it, could help. Which was true, she thought later; leaving this world clasping the hand of another was far better than going alone.

'How is the hospital?' she asked. 'I have heard that you have a lot of new things there. New beds. New X-ray machines.'

'We have all of that,' said Tati Monyena. 'The Government has been very generous.'

'It is your money,' chipped in Mma Makutsi from behind his chair. 'When people say that the Government has given them this thing or that thing, they are forgetting that the thing which the Government gave them belonged to the people in the first place!' She paused, and then added, 'Everybody knows that.'

In the silence that followed, a small white gecko, one of those albino-like creatures that cling to walls and ceilings, defying gravity with their tiny sucker-like toes, ran across a section of ceiling board. Two flies, which had landed on the same section, moved, but languidly, to escape the approaching danger. Mma Ramotswe's gaze followed the gecko, but then dropped to Mma Makutsi, sitting defiantly below. What she said might be true—in fact, it was self-evidently true—but she should not have used that disparaging tone, as if Tati Monyena were a schoolboy who

27

needed the facts of public finance spelled out for him.

'Rra Monyena knows all that, Mma,' said Mma Ramotswe quietly.

Tati Monyena gave a nervous glance over his shoulder in the direction of Mma Makutsi. 'What she says is right,' he said. 'It is our money.'

'You wouldn't think that some politicians knew that,' said Mma Makutsi.

Mma Ramotswe decided that it was time to get the conversation off politics. 'So the hospital wants me to do something,' she said. 'I am happy to help. But you must tell me what the problem is.'

'That's what doctors say,' offered Mma Makutsi from the other side of the office. 'They say, *What seems to be the problem?* when you go to see them. And then they say . . .'

'Thank you very much, Mma,' said Mma Ramotswe firmly. 'No, Rra, what is this problem that the hospital has?'

Tati Monyena sighed. 'I wish we had only one problem,' he began. 'In fact, we have many problems. All hospitals have problems. Not enough funds. Not enough nurses. Infection control. It would be a very big list if I were to tell you about all our problems. But there is one problem in particular that we decided I needed to ask you about. One very big problem.'

'Which is?'

'People have died in the hospital,' he said.

Mma Ramotswe caught Mma Makutsi's eye. She did not want any further remarks from that quarter, and she gave her assistant a severe look. She could imagine what Mma Makutsi might have said to that: that people were always dying in

28

hospitals, and that it was surely no cause for complaint if this happened from time to time. Hospitals were full of sick people, and sick people died if the treatment did not work.

'I am sorry,' said Mma Ramotswe. 'I can imagine that the hospital does not like its patients to become late. But, after all, hospitals . . .'

'Oh we know that we're going to lose a certain number of patients,' said Tati Monyena quickly. 'You can't avoid that.'

'So, why would you need my services?' asked Mma Ramotswe.

Tati Monyena hesitated before he replied. 'This will go no further?' he asked. His voice was barely above a whisper.

'This is a confidential consultation,' Mma Ramotswe reassured him. 'It is just between you and me. Nobody else.'

Tati Monyena looked over his shoulder again. Mma Makutsi was staring at him through her large round glasses and he quickly looked back again.

'My assistant is bound to secrecy too,' said Mma Ramotswe. 'We do not talk about our clients' affairs.'

'Except when . . .' began Mma Makutsi, but she was cut off by Mma Ramotswe, who raised her voice.

'Except never,' she said. 'Except never.'

Tati Monyena looked uncomfortable at this display of disagreement and hesitated a moment. But then he continued, 'People become late in a hospital for all sorts of reasons. You would be surprised, Mma Ramotswe, at how many patients decide that now that they've arrived in hospital it's time to go . . .' He pointed up at the ceiling. 'To go up there. And then there are those who fall out of bed and those who have a bad reaction to some drug and so on. There are many unfortunate things that happen in a hospital.

'But then there are those cases where we just don't know why somebody became late—we just don't know. There are not many of these cases, but they do happen. Sometimes I think that is because of a broken heart. That is something that you cannot see, you know. The pathologist does a post-mortem and the heart looks fine from outside. But it is broken inside, from some sadness. From being far from home, maybe, and thinking that you will never again see your family, or your cattle. That can break the heart.'

Mma Ramotswe nodded her agreement at that. She knew about broken hearts, and she understood how they can occur. Her father had told her about that many years ago; about how some men who went off to the mines in South Africa died for no reason at all, or so it seemed. A few weeks after they had arrived in Johannesburg, they simply died, because they were so far from Botswana, and their hearts were broken. She remembered that now.

'A broken heart,' mused Tati Monyena. 'But to have a broken heart you have to be awake, Mma, would you not agree?'

Mma Ramotswe looked puzzled. 'Awake?'

'Yes. Let me tell you what happened, Mma, and then you will see what I mean. I'm not sure if you know much about hospitals, but you know about a ward they have which is called intensive care. That is for people who are very ill and have to be looked after by nurses all the time, or just about all the

30

time. Sometimes these people are in comas, on ventilators, which help them to breathe. You know about those machines, Mma?'

Mma Ramotswe did.

'Well,' continued Tati Monyena, 'we have a ward like that in the hospital. And of course when people become late in that ward nobody is too surprised. They are very sick when they go in and not all of them will come out. But . . .' He raised a finger in the air to emphasise the point. 'But, when you have three deaths in six months and each of those takes place in the same bed, then you begin to wonder.'

'Coincidence,' muttered Mma Makutsi. 'There are many coincidences.'

This time, Tati Monyena did not turn to answer her, but addressed his reply to Mma Ramotswe. 'Oh, I know about coincidences,' he said. 'That could easily be a coincidence. I know that. But what if those three deaths take place at more or less exactly the same time on a Friday? All of them?' He raised three fingers in the air. 'Friday.' One finger went down. 'Friday.' The second finger. 'Friday.' The third.

CHAPTER THREE

I Have Found You

Mma Makutsi went home that day thinking about what Tati Monyena had said. She preferred not to dwell upon her work once she left the office—something that they had strongly recommended at

31

the Botswana Secretarial College. 'Don't go home and write letters all over again in your head,' said the lecturer. 'It is best to leave the problems of the office where they belong—in the office.'

She had done that, for the most part, but it was not easy when there was something as unusual—as shocking, perhaps—as this. Even though she tried to put out of her mind the account of the three unusual hospital deaths, the image returned of Tati Monyena holding up three fingers and bringing them down one by one. So might the passing of one's life be marked—by the raising and lowering of a finger. She thought of this again as she unlocked the door of her house and flicked the light switch. On, off; like our lives.

It had not been a good day for Mma Makutsi. She had not sought out that altercation with Mma Ramotswe—if one could call it that—and it had left her feeling uncomfortable. It was Mma Ramotswe's fault, she decided; she should not have made those remarks about shopping during working hours. One might reasonably require a junior clerk to keep strict hours, but when it came to those at a higher level, such as herself, then a certain leeway was surely normal. If one went to the shops in the afternoon they were full of people who were senior enough to take the time off to do their shopping. One could not expect such people—and she included herself in that category—to struggle to get everything done on a Saturday morning, when the whole town was trying to do the same thing. If Mma Ramotswe did not appreciate that, she said to herself, then she would have to employ somebody else.

She stopped. She was standing in the middle of

the room when this thought crossed her mind, and she realised that it was the first time she had seriously contemplated leaving her job. And now that she had articulated the possibility, even if only to herself, she found that she felt ashamed. Mma Ramotswe had given her her first job when she had been beaten to so many others by those feckless, glamorous girls from the Botswana Secretarial College, with their measly fifty per cent results in the final examinations. It had been Mma Ramotswe who had seen beyond that and had taken her on, even when the agency could hardly afford to pay her wages. That had been one of Mma Ramotswe's many acts of kindness, and there had been others. There had been her promotion; there had been her support after the death of her brother, Richard, when Mma Ramotswe had given her three weeks off and had paid half the cost of the funeral. She had expected and wanted no thanks, had done it out of the goodness of her heart, and here was she, Mma Makutsi, thinking of leaving simply because her circumstances had improved and she was in a position to do so. She felt a flush of shame. She would apologise to Mma Ramotswe the next day and offer to work some overtime for nothing—well perhaps not quite that, but she would make a gesture.

Mma Makutsi put the bag she was carrying on the table and started to unpack it. She had called in at the shops on the way home and had bought the supplies that she needed for Phuti Radiphuti's dinner. He came to eat at her house on several evenings a week—on the others he still ate with his father or his aunt—and she liked to prepare him something special. Of course she knew what he liked, which was meat, good beef fed on the sweet, dry grass of Botswana; beef served with rice and thick gravy and broad beans. Mma Ramotswe always liked to cook boiled pumpkin with beef, but Mma Makutsi preferred beans, and so did Phuti Radiphuti. It was a good thing, she thought, that they liked the same things, on the table and elsewhere, and that boded well for the marriage, when it eventually happened. That was something she wanted to talk to Phuti about, without appearing to be either too anxious or too keen about it. She was acutely aware of the fact that Mma Ramotswe's engagement to Mr J.L.B. Matekoni had been a long-drawn-out affair, concluded only when he was more or less manoeuvred into position for the wedding by no less a person than Mma Potokwani. She did not want her engagement to last that long, and she would have to get Phuti Radiphuti to agree to a date for the wedding. He had already spoken of that, and had shown no signs of the reluctance, dithering really, which had held back Mr J.L.B. Matekoni from naming a day.

The winter day died with the quickness of those latitudes. It seemed to be only for a few moments that the sun made the sky to the west red, and then it was gone. The night would be a cold one, clear and cold, with the stars suspended above like crystals. She looked out of her window at the lights of the neighbouring houses. Through the windows she saw her neighbours on the other side of the road seated round the fire that she knew they liked to keep going in their hearth throughout the winter months, triggering the memory, long overlaid but still there, of sitting around the fire at the cattle posts. Mma Makutsi had no fireplace in her house, but she would have, she thought, when she moved to Phuti's house, which had more than one; mantelpieces, too, on which she could put the ornaments which she currently kept in a box behind her settee. There would be so much room in her new life; room for all the things that she had been unable to do because of poverty, and if she did not have to work—that thought returned unbidden—then she would be able to do so much. And she could stay in bed, too, if she wished, until eight in the morning; such a prospect—no dashing for the minibus, no crowding with two other people into a seat made for two; and so often, it seemed, those others were ladies of traditional build who could have done with an entire bench seat to themselves.

She prepared a stew for Phuti Radiphuti and carefully measured out the beans that would accompany it. Then she laid the table with the plates that she knew he liked, the ones with the blue and red circles, with his teacup, a large one with a blue design that she had bought at the bring-and-buy sale at the Anglican Cathedral. 'That teacup,' Mma Ramotswe had said, 'belonged to the last Dean. He was such a kind man. I saw him drinking from it.'

'It belongs to me now,' said Mma Makutsi.

Like Mma Ramotswe, Phuti Radiphuti drank red bush tea, which he thought was much better for you, but he had never asked Mma Makutsi for it and had simply taken what was served to him. He was planning, though, to make the request, but the moment had not yet arisen and with each pot of ordinary tea served it became more difficult for him to ask for something different. That had been Mma Makutsi's own quandary, resolved when she had eventually plucked up all her courage and blurted out to Mma Ramotswe that she would like to have India tea and would have preferred that all along.

There were one or two other matters which Phuti Radiphuti would have liked to raise with his fiancée but which he had found himself unable to bring up. They were small things, of course, but important in a shared life. He did not take to her curtains; yellow was not a colour that appealed to him in the slightest. In his view, the best colour for curtains was undoubtedly light blue—the blue of the national flag. It was not a question of patriotism; although there were those who painted their front doors that blue for reasons of pride. And why should they not do so, when there was a lot to be proud of? It was more a question of restfulness. Blue was a peaceful colour, Phuti Radiphuti thought. Yellow, by contrast, was an energetic, unsettled colour; a colour of warning, every bit as much as red was; a colour which made one feel vaguely uncomfortable.

But when he arrived at her house that evening, he did not want to discuss curtain colour. Quite suddenly, Phuti Radiphuti felt grateful; simply relieved that of all the men she must have come across, Mma Makutsi had chosen him. She had chosen him in spite of his stammer and his inability to dance; had seen past all that and had worked with such success on both of these defects. For that he felt thankful, so thankful, in fact, that it hurt; for it so easily might have been quite different. She might have laughed at him, or simply looked away

36

with embarrassment as she heard his unco-operative tongue mangle the liquid syllables of Setswana; but she did not do that because she was a kind woman, and now she was about to become his wife.

'We must decide on a day for the wedding,' he said as he sat down at the table. 'We cannot leave that matter up in the . . .' The importance of what he was about to say made the words stick; they would not come.

'Up in the air,' said Mma Makutsi quickly.

'Yes,' he said. 'Yes. We must share . . . must share . . . our . . . our . . .'

For a moment Mma Makutsi thought that the next word was *blanket*, and almost supplied that, for this was a common metaphor in Setswana—to share a blanket. But then she realised that Phuti Radiphuti would never be so forward as to say such a thing, and she stopped herself just in time.

'Our ideas on that,' went on Phuti Radiphuti.

'Of course. We must share our ideas on that.'

Phuti Radiphuti was relieved that he had made a start and went on to deal with the details. Now he spoke easily again, with none of the stumbling that had at one time dogged him when he had something important to say.

'I think that we should get married in January,' said Phuti. 'January is a month when people are looking for things to do. A wedding will keep them busy. You know, all the aunties and people like that.'

Mma Makutsi laughed. There was so much to think of—so many exciting things—but this reference to aunts gave her a reason to chuckle. And beyond the amusement there was the heady,

37

intoxicating fact: he had said it! He may not have named a day, but at least he had named a month! Her marriage was now not just some sort of vague possibility in the future; it was a singled-out time, as definite, as cast in stone, as the dates on her calendar in the office from the Good Impression Printing Company: 30 September—Botswana Independence Day; 1 July—Birthday of Sir Seretse Khama. Those dates she remembered, as everyone did, because they were holidays, and Mma Ramotswe remembered a few more: 21 April—Queen Elizabeth II's birthday; 4 July—Independence Day of the United States of America. There were others in the calendar that the Good Impression Printing Company thought important enough to note, but which escaped the attention of the No. 1 Ladies' Detective Agency. Some of these were other national days; 1 October, for example, was Nigeria's national day, and was marked in the calendar, but not observed in any way by Mma Ramotswe. When Mma Makutsi had drawn Mma Ramotswe's attention to the significance of that day, there had been a brief silence and then, 'That may be so, Mma, and I am happy for them. But we cannot observe everybody's national day, can we, or life would be one constant celebration.' The apprentices had been hovering nearby when this remark was passed and Charlie, the older one, had opened his mouth to say, 'And what would be wrong with that?' but had stopped himself and instead nodded his head in exaggerated agreement.

She sat quite still at the table, her eyes lowered to the plate before her. 'Yes. January would be a good time. That gives people six months to get

38

ready. That should be enough.'

Phuti agreed. It had always struck him as strange that people took such trouble over weddings, with two parties—one for each family—and a great deal of coming and going by anybody who was related, even distantly, to the couple. Six months would be reasonable, and would not encourage unnecessary activity; if one allowed a year, then people would think of a year's worth of things to do.

'You have an uncle . . .' he began. This, he knew, was the delicate part of the matter. Mma Makutsi would have to be paid for, and an uncle would probably wish to negotiate the bride price. Her uncle would speak to his father and his uncles, and together they would agree the figure, notionally in head of cattle.

He stole a glance at his fiancée. A woman of her education and talents could expect a fairly good dowry—perhaps nine cattle—even if her background would not normally justify more than seven or eight. But would this uncle, if he existed, try to raise the price once he found out about the Double Comfort Furniture Store and all those Radiphuti cattle out at the cattle post? In Phuti Radiphuti's experience, uncles did their homework in these situations.

'Yes,' said Mma Makutsi. 'I have an uncle. He is my senior uncle and I think that he will want to talk about these things.'

It was delicately put, and it made it possible for Phuti Radiphuti to move on from this potentially awkward topic to the safer ground of food. 'I know somebody who is a very good caterer,' he said. 'She has a truck with a fridge in it. She is very good at this sort of thing.'

39

'She sounds just right,' said Mma Makutsi.

'And I can get hold of chairs for the guests to sit on,' went on Phuti Radiphuti.

Of course, thought Mma Makutsi; the Double Comfort Furniture Store would come in useful for that. There was nothing worse than a wedding where there were not enough chairs for people to sit on and they ended up eating with their plates balanced on all sorts of things, ant heaps even, and getting food on their smart clothes. She vowed to herself, that will not happen at my wedding, and the thought filled her with pride. *My wedding. My wedding guests. Chairs.* It was a long way from those days of penury as a student at the Botswana Secretarial College, of rationing herself in what she ate; of making do with just one of anything, if that. Well, those days were over now.

And Phuti Radiphuti, for his part, thought, *My days of loneliness are finished. My days of being laughed at because of the way I speak and because no woman would look at me—those are over now. Those are over.*

He reached out and took Mma Makutsi's hand. She smiled at him. 'I am very lucky to have found you,' he said.

'No, I am the lucky one. I am the one.'

He thought that unlikely, but he was moved very deeply that somebody should consider herself lucky to have him, of all people. The previously unloved may find it hard to believe that they are now loved; that is such a miracle, they feel; such a miracle.

*   *   *

40

While Mma Makutsi and Phuti Radiphuti were reflecting on their good fortune, Mma Ramotswe and Mr J.L.B. Matekoni, who themselves had on many occasions pondered their own good luck, were engaged in a conversation of an entirely different nature. They had finished their dinner and the children had been dispatched to bed. Both were tired—he because he had removed an entire engine that afternoon, a task which involved considerable physical exertion, and she because she had awoken the night before and lost an hour or two of sleep. The kitchen clock, which always ran ten minutes fast, revealed that it was eight thirty, eight twenty after adjustment. One could not decently go to bed before eight thirty, Mma Ramotswe felt; and so she sat back and chatted with her husband about the day's events. She was not particularly interested in the removal of the engine, and listened to his comments on that with only half an ear. But then he said something which engaged her full attention.

'That woman I spoke to,' he said. 'Mma what's-her-name. The one with the husband.'

'Mma Botumile.' Mma Ramotswe's tone was cautious.

'Yes, her,' said Mr J.L.B. Matekoni. 'I thought that maybe . . . that maybe because I spoke to her first . . .' He trailed off. Mma Ramotswe was staring at him, and he felt disconcerted.

Mma Ramotswe thought for a while before she said anything. It was important that she should handle this carefully. 'Do you want to be involved?' she asked.

'I already am,' he said.

She hesitated. 'In a way.'

41

Mr J.L.B. Matekoni now became more confident. 'Being a mechanic is fine,' he said. 'But it is always the same thing. A car comes in, I listen to what the engine has to say, I make my diagnosis, and then I fix it. That is what I do.'

There was nothing wrong with that, thought Mma Ramotswe. Being a mechanic was a great calling, in her view, and was certainly more useful than many of the white-collar jobs that seemed to carry all the prestige. A country could never have too many mechanics, but it could have too many of the civil servants who wrote complicated and obscure letters to Mma Ramotswe about her tax payments and about various forms and returns that they thought she should fill in.

It worried her that Mr J.L.B. Matekoni should find his work repetitive. Everybody's work was repetitive, if one thought about it, even in a business such as the No. 1 Ladies' Detective Agency there was a certain sameness to the enquiries that she and Mma Makutsi undertook. Was so-and-so being unfaithful? Was some dispatch clerk making up bogus orders and then claiming that the invoices were lost? Were somebody's impressive work record and testimonials entirely false? The same things arose time and time again, even if there were features of some cases that made them particularly amusing. That testimonial, for example, that she had been asked to check a few months ago where the writing was almost illegible and where the final sentence said, *I have never heard this person use strong language, even to himself.* Did anybody seriously imagine that real testimonials said things like that? Obviously somebody did think that. What might she write—in that style—of Mma Makutsi, if she had to write her a testimonial? *She divides the office doughnuts with complete impartiality.* That would be a good recommendation, she thought; how a person divided a shared doughnut was a real test of integrity. A good person would cut the doughnut into two equal pieces. A shifty, selfish person would divide it into two pieces, but one would be bigger than the other and he would take that one himself. She had seen that happen.

No, every job had its repetitive side and most people, surely, recognised that. She glanced again at Mr J.L.B. Matekoni. She knew that many men of his age started to feel trapped and began to wonder if this was all that life offered. It was understandable; anyone might feel that, not just men, although they might feel it particularly acutely, as they felt themselves weaken and began to realise that they were no longer young. Women were better at coming to terms with that, thought Mma Ramotswe, as long as they were not the worrying sort. If one was of traditional build and not given to fretting . . . If one drank plenty of bush tea . . .

'You know,' she said to Mr J.L.B. Matekoni, 'all of us have things that are the same in our jobs. Even in the sort of work I do, the same sort of thing happens quite a lot. I don't think there is anything much that you can do.'

It was not like Mr J.L.B. Matekoni to argue, but now, if there was a stubborn streak in his character, it showed. 'No,' he said. 'I think there is something that you can do. You can try something different.'

Mma Ramotswe was silent. She reached for her

teacup. It was cold. She looked at him. It was inconceivable that Mr J.L.B. Matekoni could be anything but a mechanic; he was a truly great mechanic, a man who understood engines, who knew their every mood. She tried to picture him in the garb of some other profession—in a banker's suit, for example, or in the white coat of a doctor, but neither of these seemed right, and she saw him again in his mechanic's overalls, in his old suede boots so covered in grease, and that somehow rang true, that was just what he should wear.

Mr J.L.B. Matekoni broke the silence. 'I'm not thinking of stopping being a mechanic, of course. Certainly not. I know that I must do that to put bread on our table.'

Mma Ramotswe's relief showed, and this caused him to smile reassuringly. 'It's just that I would like to do a little bit of detective work. Not much. Just a little.'

That, she thought, was reasonable enough. She had no desire to fix engines, but there was no harm in his wanting to see her side of the business. 'Just to find out what it's like? Just to get it out of your system?' she asked, smiling. Most men, she thought, fantasised about doing something exciting, about being a soldier, or a secret agent, or even a great lover; that was how men were. That was normal.

Mr J.L.B. Matekoni frowned. 'Please don't laugh at me, Mma Ramotswe.'

She leaned forward and rested her hand on his forearm. 'I would never laugh at you, Mr J.L.B. Matekoni. I would never do that. And of course you can look after a case. How about this Mma Botumile matter? Would that do?'

'That is the one that I want to investigate,' he said. 'That is the one.'

'Then you shall investigate,' she said.

Even as she spoke, she had her misgivings, unexpressed. The thought of Mma Botumile's reputation disturbed her, and she was not sure whether she should put Mr J.L.B. Matekoni in the path of a woman like that. But it was too late to do anything about it, and so she looked at her watch and rose to her feet. She would not think about it any more, or she would have difficulty in getting to sleep.

CHAPTER FOUR

Mma Ramotswe goes to Mochudi with Mr Polopetsi, in the Tiny White Van

Mma Ramotswe travelled to Mochudi the next day. She decided to take Mr Polopetsi with her; there was nothing for him to do in the garage that morning and he had asked Mma Makutsi three times if there was anything that he could help her with in the office. She had tried to think of some task, and failed, and so Mma Ramotswe had invited him to accompany her on the Mochudi trip. She enjoyed his company, and it would be good to have somebody to talk to. Whether he would contribute anything to her enquiries there was another matter; Mr Polopetsi, she feared, would never distinguish himself in the role of detective, as he tended to jump to conclusions and to act impetuously. But there was something appealing about him that made all that forgivable—an earnestness combined with a slight air of vulnerability that made people, particularly women, want to protect him. Even Mma Makutsi, who was famously short with the two apprentices and who tended to talk to men as if they were children, had been won over by Mr Polopetsi. 'There are many men for whom there does not appear to be any reason,' she once said to Mma Ramotswe. 'But I don't feel that about Mr Polopetsi. Even when he is standing there, doing nothing, I don't think that.'

It had been a curious thing to say, but then Mma Makutsi often said things that surprised Mma Ramotswe and she had become used to her pronouncements. But what made this remark particularly unusual was the fact that it was made while Mr Polopetsi was in the office, busying himself with the making of a pot of tea. Mma Makutsi must have been aware of his coming into the room, but must simply have forgotten his presence after a few moments and addressed Mma Ramotswe without thinking. And there was no doubt in Mma Ramotswe's mind that Mr Polopetsi had heard what was said about him, for he stopped stirring the tea for a moment, as if frozen, and then, after a few seconds, began to rattle the spoon about the pot more vigorously than before. Mma Ramotswe had felt acutely embarrassed, but had decided that the remark was hardly unflattering to Mr Polopetsi, even if he had scurried out of the room, his mug of tea in his hand, studiously avoiding looking at the author of the remark. For Mma Makutsi's part, she had simply raised an eyebrow when she realised that he had heard her, and shrugged, as if this was merely one of those

46

things that happened in offices.

They drove out to Mochudi on the old road, because that was the way that Mma Ramotswe had always travelled and because it was quieter. It was a bright morning, and there was warmth in the air; not the heat that would come in a month or so and build up over the final months of the year, but a pleasant feeling of a benign sun upon the skin. As they left Gaborone behind them, the houses and their surrounding plots gave way to the bush, to the expanses of dry grass dotted with acacia and smaller thorn bushes that were halfway between trees and shrubs. Here and there was a dry river bed, a scar of sand that would remain parched until the rainy season, when it would be covered with swift-moving dun-coloured water, a proper river for a few days until it all drained off and the bed would cake and crack in the sun.

For a while they did not talk. Mma Ramotswe looked out of the window of her tiny white van, savouring the feeling of heading somewhere she was always happy to be going; for Mochudi was home, the place from which she had come and to which she knew that she would one day return for good. Mr Polopetsi looked straight ahead, at the road unfolding ahead of them, lost in thoughts of his own. He was waiting for Mma Ramotswe to tell him about the reason for their trip to Mochudi; she had simply said at the office that she needed to go there and would tell him all about it on the way up.

He glanced at her sideways. 'This business . . .'

Mma Ramotswe was thinking of something quite different, of this road and of how she had once travelled down it by bus, unhappy to the very core of her being; but that was years ago, years. She moved her hands on the wheel. 'We don't usually get involved in cases where people have died, Rra,' she said. 'We may be detectives, but not that sort.'

Mr Polopetsi drew in his breath. Ever since he had joined the staff of the No. 1 Ladies' Detective Agency—even in his ill-defined adjunct role—he had been waiting for something like this. Murder was what detectives were meant to investigate, was it not, and now at last they were embarked on such an enquiry.

'Murder,' he whispered. 'There have been murders?'

Mma Ramotswe was about to laugh at the suggestion. 'Oh no,' she began. But then she stopped herself and the thought occurred to her that perhaps this was exactly what they were letting themselves in for. Tati Monyena had described the deaths as *mishaps* and had hinted, at the most, that there was some form of unexplained negligence behind them; he had said nothing about deliberate killing. And yet it was possible, was it not? She remembered reading somewhere about cases where hospital patients had been deliberately killed by doctors or nurses. She thought hard, probing the recesses of her memory, and it came to her. Yes, there had been such a doctor in Zimbabwe, in Bulawayo, and she had read about him. He had started to poison people while he was still at medical school in America and had continued to do so for years. These people existed. Was it possible that a person like that could have slipped into Botswana? Or could it be a nurse? They did it too sometimes, she believed. It gave them power, somebody had said. They felt powerful.

She half-turned to Mr Polopetsi. 'I hope not,' she said. 'But we must keep an open mind, Rra. It is possible, I suppose.'

They were ten miles from Mochudi now, and Mma Ramotswe spent the rest of the journey describing to Mr Polopetsi what Tati Monyena had told her: three Fridays, three unexplained deaths, and all in the same bed.

'That cannot be a coincidence,' he said, shaking his head. 'That sort of thing just does not happen.' He paused. 'You know that I worked in this hospital once, Mma Ramotswe? Did I tell you that?'

Mma Ramotswe knew that Mr Polopetsi had worked as an assistant in the pharmacy at the Princess Marina Hospital in Gaborone, and she knew of the injustice that occurred there which led to his spell in prison. But she did not know that he had been at Mochudi.

'Yes,' Mr Polopetsi explained. 'I was there for eight months, while they were short-staffed. That was about four years ago. I was in the pharmacy.' He lowered his voice as he mentioned the pharmacy, in shame, she thought. All that had turned sour for him, and all because of a lying witness and the transfer of blame. It was so unfair, but she had gone over all that with him before, several times, and she knew—they both knew— that they could do nothing to remedy it. 'You are innocent in your heart,' she had said to him. 'That is the most important thing.' And he had thought about that for a few moments before shaking his head and saying, 'I would like that to be true, Mma, but it is not. It is what other people think. *That* is the most important thing.'

49

Now, as they made their way through the outskirts of Mochudi, past the rash of small hairdressing establishments with their hand-painted grandiose signs, past the turn-offs that led to the larger houses of those who had made good in Gaborone and returned to the village, past the tax office and the general dealers, he said to her casually, almost as if he were thinking aloud, 'I wouldn't like to be one of his patients.'

'Of whose patients?'

'There was a doctor who worked at the hospital when I was there,' he said. 'I didn't like him. Nobody did. And I remember thinking: I would be frightened to be in that doctor's care. I really would.'

She changed gear. A donkey had wandered onto the road and was standing directly in the path of the tiny white van. It was a defeated, cowed creature, and seemed to be looking directly up at the sun.

'That donkey is blind,' said Mr Polopetsi. 'Look at him.'

She guided the van round the static animal. 'Why?' she said.

'Why does he stand there? That is what they do. That is just the way they are.'

'No,' she said. 'That is not what I meant. I wondered what frightened you about him.'

He thought for a few moments before answering. 'You get a feeling sometimes. You just do.' He paused. 'Maybe we'll see him.'

'Is he still here, Rra?'

Mr Polopetsi shrugged. 'He was last year. I heard from a friend. I don't know if he has moved since then. Maybe not. He was married to a

50

woman from Mochudi, so maybe he will still be here. He is a South African himself. Xhosa mother, Boer father.'

Mma Ramotswe was thoughtful. 'Do you know many others from the hospital staff? From that time?'

'Many,' said Mr Polopetsi.

Mma Ramotswe nodded. It had been a good idea, she decided, to bring Mr Polopetsi with her. Clovis Andersen, author of *The Principles of Private Detection*, said in one of his chapters that there was no substitute for local knowledge. *It cuts hours and days off an investigation*, he wrote. *Local knowledge is like gold.*

Mma Ramotswe glanced at her modest assistant. It was difficult to think of Mr Polopetsi in these golden terms; he was so mild and diffident. But Clovis Andersen was usually right about these things, and she muttered *gold* under her breath.

'What?' asked Mr Polopetsi.

'We have arrived,' said Mma Ramotswe.

*   *   *

Tati Monyena was clearly proud of his office, which was scrupulously clean and which exuded the smell of polish. In the centre of the room stood a large desk on which rested a telephone, three stacked letter trays, and a small wooden sign, facing out, on which was inscribed *Mr T. Monyena*. Against one wall stood two grey metal filing cabinets, considerably more modern than those in Mma Ramotswe's office, and on another wall, directly behind Tati Monyena's chair was a large framed picture of His Excellency, the President of the Republic of Botswana.

Mma Ramotswe and Mr Polopetsi sat in the straight-backed chairs in front of the desk. It was a tight fit for Mma Ramotswe, and the chair-arm on each side pushed uncomfortably into her traditional waistline. Mr Polopetsi, though, barely filled his seat, and perched nervously on the edge of it, his hands clasped together on his lap.

'It is very good of you to come so quickly,' said Tati Monyena. 'We are at your disposal.' He paused. He had made a magnanimous beginning, but he was not at all sure what he could do to help Mma Ramotswe. She would want to speak to people, he imagined, even though he had spoken to the ward nurses again and again, and had had several conversations with the doctors in question, in this very office; conversations in which the doctors sat where Mma Ramotswe was sitting and defensively insisted that they had no idea how these patients had died.

'I should like to speak to the nurses,' said Mma Ramotswe. 'And I should like to see the ward too, if possible.'

Tati Monyena's hand reached for the telephone. 'I can arrange for both of those things, Mma. I shall show you the ward, and then we will bring the nurses back here so you can talk to them in this office. There are three of them who were there at the time.'

Mma Ramotswe frowned. She did not wish to be rude, but it would not be a good idea to interview the nurses in front of Tati Monyena. 'It might be better for me to see them by themselves,' she said. 'Just Mr Polopetsi here and myself. That's not to suggest . . .'

Tati Monyena raised a hand to stop her. 'Of course, Mma! Of course. How tactless of me! You can speak to them in private. But I don't think they will say anything. When things go wrong, people become very careful. They forget what they have seen. They saw nothing. Nothing happened. It is always the same thing.'

'That is human nature,' interjected Mr Polopetsi. He had been silent until then, and they both looked at him intently.

'Of course it is,' said Tati Monyena. 'It is human nature to protect ourselves. We are no different from animals in that respect.'

'Except that they can't tell lies,' said Mr Polopetsi.

Tati Monyena laughed. 'Of course. But that's only because they cannot speak. I think that if they could, then they would probably lie too. Would a dog own up if some meat had been stolen? Would it say, *I am the one who has eaten the meat*? I do not think so.'

Mma Ramotswe wondered whether to join in this speculative conversation, but decided against it, and sat back until the two of them should finish. But Tati Monyena rose to his feet instead and gestured towards the door. 'I shall take you to the ward,' he said. 'You will see the bed where these things happened.'

They left his office and walked down a green-painted corridor. There was a hospital smell in the air, that mixture of humanity and disinfectant, and, in the background, the sound that seemed to go so well with that smell—voices somewhere, the sound of a child crying, the noise of wheels being pushed over uneven floors, the faint hum of machinery.

There were posters on the wall: warnings about disease and the need to be careful; a picture of a blood spill. This, ultimately, was what our life was about, she thought, and hospitals were there to remind us: biology, human need, human suffering.

They passed a nurse in the corridor. She was carrying a pan of some sort, covered with a stained cloth, and she smiled and half-turned to let them pass. Mma Ramotswe kept her gaze studiously away from the pan and on the nurse's face. It was a kind face, the sort that one trusted, unlike, she imagined, the face of the doctor whom Mr Polopetsi had described.

'It's changed since your father was here,' said Tati Monyena. 'In those days we had to make do with so little. Now we have much more.'

'But there is never enough, is there?' said Mr Polopetsi. 'We get drugs for one illness and then a new illness comes along. Or a new type of the same thing. Same devil, different clothes. Look at TB.'

Tati Monyena sighed. 'That is true. I was talking to one of the doctors the other day and he said, *We thought that we had it cracked. We really did. And now . . .*'

But at least we can try, thought Mma Ramotswe. That is all we can do. We can try. And that, surely, is what doctors did. They did not throw up their hands and give up; they tried.

They turned a corner. A small boy, three or four years old, wearing only a vest, his tiny stomach protruding in a small mound, his eyes wide, stood in their way. The hospital was full of such children, the offspring of patients or patients themselves, and Tati Monyena barely saw him. But the child looked at Mma Ramotswe and came up to her and reached for her hand, as children will, especially in Africa, where they will still come to you. She bent down and lifted him up. He looked at her and snuggled his head against her chest.

'The mother of that one is late,' said Tati Monyena in a matter-of-fact voice. 'Our people are deciding what to do. The nurses are looking after him.'

The child looked up at Mma Ramotswe. She saw that his eyes were shallow; there was no light in them. His skin, she felt, was dry.

Tati Monyena waited for her to put the child down. Then he indicated towards a further corridor to the right. 'It is this way,' he said.

The ward doors were open. It was a long room, with six beds on either side. At the far end of the room, at a desk with several cabinets about it, a nurse was sitting, looking at a piece of paper with another nurse who was leaning over her shoulder. Halfway down the ward, another couple of nurses were adjusting the sheets on one of the beds, propping up the patient against a high bank of pillows. A drugs trolley stood unattended at the foot of another bed, an array of small containers on its top shelf.

When she saw them at the door, the nurse at the desk rose to her feet and walked down the ward to meet them. She nodded to Mma Ramotswe and Mr Polopetsi and then looked enquiringly at Tati Monyena.

'This lady is dealing with that ... that matter,' said Tati Monyena, nodding at the bed on his left. 'I spoke to you about her.' He turned to Mma Ramotswe. 'This is Sister Batshegi.'

Mma Ramotswe was watching the nurse's

expression. She knew that the first moments were the significant ones, and that people gave away so much before they had time to think and to compose themselves. Sister Batshegi had looked down, not meeting Mma Ramotswe's gaze, and then had looked up again. Did that mean anything? Mma Ramotswe thought that it meant that she was not particularly pleased to see her. But that in itself did not tell her very much. People who are busy with some task—as Sister Batshegi clearly had been—were not always pleased to be disturbed.

'I am happy to see you, Mma,' said Sister Batshegi.

Mma Ramotswe replied to the greeting and then turned to Tati Monyena. 'That is the bed, Rra?'

'It is.' He looked at Sister Batshegi. 'Have you had anybody in it over the last few days?'

The nurse shook her head. 'There has been nobody. The last patient was that man last week— the one who had the motorcycle accident near Pilane. He got better quickly.' She turned to Mma Ramotswe. 'Every time I see a motorcyle, Mma, I think of the young men we get in here ...' She shrugged. 'But they never think of that. They don't.'

'Young men often don't think,' said Mma Ramotswe. 'They cannot help it. That is how they are.' She thought of the apprentices, and reflected on what a good illustration they were of the proposition she had just made. But they would start to think sooner or later, she told herself; even Charlie would start to think. She looked at the bed, covered in its neat white sheet. Although the sheet was clean, there were brown stains on it, the stains

56

of blood that the hospital laundry could not remove. At the top of the bed, to the side, she saw a machine with tubes and dials on a stand.

'That is a ventilator,' said Tati Monyena. 'It helps people to breathe. All three patients . . .' He paused, and looked at Sister Batshegi, as if for confirmation. 'All three patients were on it at the time. But the machine was thoroughly checked and there was nothing wrong with it.'

Sister Batshegi nodded. 'The machine was working. And we checked the alarm. It has a battery, which was working fine. If the machine had been faulty we would have known.'

'So you can rule out a defective ventilator,' said Tati Monyena. 'That is not what caused it.'

Sister Batshegi was vigorously of the same mind. 'No. It is not that. That is not what happened.'

Mma Ramotswe looked about her. One of the patients at the end of the ward was calling out, a cracked, unhappy voice. A nurse went over to the bed quickly.

'I have to get on with my work,' said Sister Batshegi. 'You may look round, Mma, but you will find nothing. There is nothing to see in this place. It is just a ward. That is all.'

*   *   *

Mma Ramotswe and Mr Polopetsi spoke to Sister Batshegi again, along with two other nurses, in Tati Monyena's office. He had left them alone, as he had promised, but through the window they saw him hovering around anxiously in the courtyard outside, looking at his watch and fiddling with a line of pens that he had clipped in his shirt pocket.

57

Sister Batshegi said little more than she had said in the ward, and the other two nurses, both of whom had been on duty at the time of the incidents, seemed very unwilling to say much at all. The deaths had been a surprise, they said, but they often lost very ill patients. Neither had been close by at the time, they said, although they were quick to point out that they were both keeping a close watch on the patients involved. 'If anything had happened, we would have known it,' said one of the nurses. 'It is not our fault, you see, Mma. It is just not our fault.'

It did not take long to interview them, and then Mma Ramotswe and Mr Polopetsi were alone in the office before Tati Monyena came back.

'Those nurses were scared about something,' said Mr Polopetsi. 'Did you see the way they looked? Did you hear it in their voices?'

Mma Ramotswe had to agree. 'But what are they scared of?' she asked.

Mr Polopetsi thought for a moment. 'They are scared of some person,' he said. 'Some unknown person is frightening them.'

'Sister Batshegi?'

'No. Not her.'

'Then who else is there? Tati Monyena?'

Mr Polopetsi did not think this likely. 'I think that he is somebody who would protect his staff rather than punish them,' he said. 'Tati Monyena is a kind man.'

'Well, I don't know what to think,' said Mma Ramotswe. 'But it's time for us to leave anyway. I don't think that there is anything more we can do here.'

They drove back to Gaborone. They spoke to

each other on the journey, but not about the visit to the hospital, as neither had much to say about that. Mr Polopetsi told Mma Ramotswe about one of his sons, who was turning out to be very good at mental arithmetic. 'He is like a calculator,' he said. 'He is already doing calculations that I cannot do, and he is only eight.'

'You must be very proud of him,' said Mma Ramotswe.

Mr Polopetsi beamed with pleasure. 'I am, Mma,' he said. 'He is the most precious thing I have in this world.' He seemed about to say something else, but stopped. He looked at Mma Ramotswe hesitantly, and she knew that he was about to make a request. It will be for money, she thought. There will be school fees to be paid, or shoes to be bought for this boy, or even a blanket; children needed all these things, all the time.

'He needs a godmother,' said Mr Polopetsi. 'He had a godmother, and now she is late. He needs a new one.'

There was only one answer Mma Ramotswe could give. 'Yes,' she said. 'I will do that, Rra.'

There would be birthdays from now on, as well as shoes and school fees and so forth. But we cannot always choose whose lives will become entangled with our own; these things happen to us, come to us uninvited, and Mma Ramotswe understood that well. And just as she had not chosen Mr Polopetsi's son, she reflected, so too had the boy not chosen her.

CHAPTER FIVE

Resignation Shoes

Mma Makutsi was eager for a report the next day. She would have preferred to have gone to Mochudi in the place of Mr Polopetsi, who she thought would not have been likely to add very much to the investigation. But she was cautious about giving offence to Mma Ramotswe after the misunderstandings of the previous day and she kept those feelings to herself. In fact, she went further than that and told Mma Ramotswe what a good idea it had been to take Mr Polopetsi. 'If you're a woman, sometimes people don't take you seriously enough,' she said. 'That is when it is useful to have a man around.'

Mma Ramotswe was non-committal about that. Men were learning, she thought, and a great deal had changed. Mma Makutsi, perhaps, was fighting battles which had already been largely won, at least in the towns. It was different in the villages, of course, where men still thought that they could do what they liked. But she was thinking of other things: she had been pondering Mr J.L.B. Matekoni's planned investigation and was wondering whether she could discreetly suggest that Mma Makutsi assist him. She could try that, certainly, but she was not sure whether he would welcome it; in fact, she was sure that he would not. Mr J.L.B. Matekoni might not be the most assertive of men, but there were sensitivities there that surfaced from time to time.

'Be that as it may,' she said to Mma Makutsi, as they began to attend to the morning mail. 'There was not very much that we could find out at the hospital. I saw the ward where it happened. I spoke to the nurses, who said almost nothing. And that was it.'

Mma Makutsi thought for a moment. 'And what can you do now?' she asked.

It was difficult for Mma Ramotswe to answer that. She very rarely gave up on a case, as solutions had a habit of cropping up as long as one was patient. But it was difficult at any particular point to say what would happen next. 'I shall wait,' she said. 'There is no special hurry, Mma. I shall wait and see what happens.'

'Well, I don't see what can possibly happen,' said Mma Makutsi. 'These things don't solve themselves, you know.'

Mma Ramotswe bit her lip and turned to the letter she had just opened. It was a letter of thanks from the parents of a young man whom she had eventually located in Francistown. There had been a family row and he had gone missing, leaving no address. There had been a girlfriend, about whom the parents knew nothing, and the young woman had eventually confided to Mma Ramotswe that he was in Francistown, although she was not sure exactly where. So Mma Ramotswe had quizzed her about his interests, which, she revealed, included jazz. From that it was a simple step to enquire of the only place in Francistown where jazz was played. Yes, they knew of him, and yes he would be playing the following evening. Would she like to come? She would not, but the young man's parents did, and they were reunited with their son. He had wanted to contact them, but was too proud; the fact that his parents had come all the way from Gaborone meant that honour was satisfied. Everybody forgave one another and started again, which, Mma Ramotswe reflected, is how many of the world's problems might be solved. We should forgive one another and start all over again. But what if those who needed to be forgiven hung on to the things that they had wrongly acquired: what then? That, she decided, was a matter that would require further thought.

'It is so easy to thank people,' said Mma Ramotswe, passing the letter over to Mma Makutsi. 'And most people don't bother to do it. They don't thank the person who does something for them. They just take it for granted.'

Mma Makutsi looked out of the window. Mma Ramotswe had done her plenty of favours in the past, and she had never written to thank her. Could the remark be aimed at her? Could Mma Ramotswe have been harbouring a grudge, as people did, sometimes for years and years? She looked at her employer and decided that this was unlikely. Mma Ramotswe could not harbour a grudge *convincingly*; she would start to laugh, or offer the object of her grudge a cup of tea, or do something which indicated that the grudge was not real.

Mma Makutsi read the letter. 'Where shall I file this, Mma?' she asked. 'We do not have a file for letters of thanks. We have a file for letters of complaint, of course. Should it go there?'

Mma Ramotswe did not think this a good idea. They could open a new file, but their filing cabinets were already overcrowded and she did not think it would be worthwhile opening a file which might never contain another letter. 'We can throw it away now,' she said.

Mma Makutsi frowned. 'At the Botswana Secretarial College we were taught never to throw anything away for at least a week,' she said. 'There might always be some follow-up.'

'There will be no follow-up to a letter of thanks,' said Mma Ramotswe. 'That is it. There will be no more. That case is closed.'

With a slow show of reluctance, Mma Makutsi held the letter over the bin and dropped it in. As she did so, the door of the office opened and Charlie, the older of the two apprentices, walked in. He had removed his work overalls to reveal a pair of jeans and a tee-shirt underneath. The tee-shirt, Mma Ramotswe noticed, had a picture of a jet aircraft on it and the slogan underneath in large letters: HIGH FLIER.

Mma Makutsi looked at him. 'Finishing work early today?' she asked. 'Ten o'clock in the morning? You're a quick worker, Charlie!'

The young man ignored this comment as he sauntered over to Mma Ramotswe's desk. 'Mma Ramotswe,' he said. 'You've always been kind to me.' He paused, casting a glance over his shoulder in the direction of Mma Makutsi. 'Now I've come to say goodbye. I'm finishing work here soon. I'm going. I've come to say goodbye.'

Mma Ramotswe stared at Charlie in astonishment. 'But you haven't finished your . . . your . . .'

'Apprenticeship,' supplied Mma Makutsi from the other side of the room. 'You silly boy! You can't leave before you've finished that.'

Charlie did not react to this. He continued to look at Mma Ramotswe. 'I haven't finished my apprenticeship—I know that,' he said. 'But you only need to finish your apprenticeship if you want to be a mechanic. Who said I want to be a mechanic?'

'You did!' shouted Mma Makutsi. 'When you signed your apprenticeship contract, you said that you wanted to be a mechanic. That's what those contracts say, you know.'

Mma Ramotswe raised a hand in a calming gesture. 'You needn't shout at him, Mma,' she said quietly. 'He is going to explain, aren't you, Charlie?'

'I'm not deaf, you know,' said Charlie over his shoulder. 'And I wasn't talking to you, anyway. There are two ladies in this room—Mma Ramotswe and . . . and another one. I was talking to Mma Ramotswe.' He turned back to face Mma Ramotswe. 'I'm going to do another job, Mma. I am going into business.'

'Business!' chuckled Mma Makutsi. 'You'll be needing a secretary soon, I suppose.'

'And don't bother to apply for that job, Mma,' Charlie snapped. 'Seventy-nine per cent or not, I would never give you a job. I'm not mad, you see.'

'Ninety-seven per cent!' shouted Mma Makutsi. 'See! You can't even get your figures right. Some profit you'll make!'

'Please do not shout at each other,' said Mma Ramotswe. 'Shouting achieves nothing. It just makes the person doing the shouting hoarse and the person being shouted at cross. That is all it does.'

'I was not shouting,' said Charlie. 'Somebody

64

else was doing the shouting. Somebody with big round glasses. Not me.'

Mma Ramotswe sighed. It was Mma Makutsi's fault, this feeling between the two of them. She was older than Charlie and might have turned a blind eye to the young man's faults; she might have encouraged him to be a bit better than he was; she might have understood that young men are like this and that one has to be tolerant.

'Tell me about this business, Charlie,' she said gently. 'What is it?'

Charlie sat down on the chair in front of Mma Ramotswe. Then he leaned forward, his arms resting on the surface of her desk. 'Mr J.L.B. Matekoni has sold me a car,' he said, his voice barely above a whisper, so that Mma Makutsi might not hear. 'It is an old Mercedes-Benz. An E220. The owner has a new one, a C class, and since this one has such a large mileage on it he sold it to the boss for very little. Twenty thousand pula. Now the boss has sold it to me.'

'And?' coaxed Mma Ramotswe. She had seen the Mercedes in the garage and had noticed that it had been parked at the side of the building for over two weeks. She assumed that they were waiting for some part that had been ordered from South Africa. Now she knew that there were other plans for the car.

'And I am going to start a taxi service,' said Charlie. 'I am going to start a business called the No. 1 Ladies' Taxi Service.'

There was a gasp from the other side of the room. 'You can't do that! That name belongs to Mma Ramotswe.'

Mma Ramotswe, taken aback, simply stared at

65

Charlie. Then she gathered her thoughts. The name that he had chosen was certainly derivative, but was there anything wrong with that? In one view, it was a compliment to have a name one had invented being used by somebody else. The only difficulty would be if the name were to be used by a similar business—by a detective agency that wanted to take clients away from them. A taxi company and a detective agency were two very different things, and there would be no prospect of competition between them.

'I don't mind,' she said to Charlie. 'But tell me: why have you chosen that name? You'll be driving the car—where do the ladies come into it?'

Charlie, who had been tense under Mma Makutsi's onslaught, now visibly relaxed. 'The ladies will be in the back of the car.'

Mma Ramotswe raised an eyebrow. 'And?'

'And I will be in the front, driving,' he said. 'The selling point will be that this is a taxi that is safe for ladies. Ladies will be able to get in without any fear that they will find some bad man in the driver's seat—a man who might not be safe with ladies. There are such taxi drivers, Mma.'

For a minute or so nobody spoke. Mma Ramotswe was aware of the sound of Charlie's breathing, which was shallow, from excitement. We must remember, she thought, what it is like to be young and enthusiastic, to have a plan, a dream. There was always a danger that as we went on in life we forgot about that; caution—even fear— replaced optimism and courage. When you were young, like Charlie, you believed that you could do anything, and, in some circumstances at least, you could.

Why should Charlie's taxi firm not succeed? She remembered a conversation with her friend, Bernard Ditau, who had been a bank manager. 'There are so many people who could run their own businesses,' he had said, 'but they let people tell them it won't work. So they give up before they start.'

Bernard had encouraged her to start the No. 1 Ladies' Detective Agency when others had merely laughed and said that it would be the quickest way of losing the money that Obed Ramotswe had left her. 'He worked all those years, your Daddy, and now you're going to lose everything he got in two or three months,' somebody had said. That remark had almost persuaded her to drop the idea, but Bernard had urged her on. 'What if he hadn't bought all those good fat cattle?' he asked. 'What if he had been too timid to do that and had left the money to sit gathering dust?'

Now she was sitting, in a sense, in Bernard's place. There was little doubt but that Mma Makutsi would be only too ready to throw cold water over Charlie's plan, but she decided that she would not do this.

'I will tell all my friends to use your taxi,' she said. 'I am sure you will be very busy.'

Charlie beamed with pleasure. 'I will give them a discount,' he said. 'Ten per cent off for anybody who knows Mma Ramotswe.'

Mma Ramotswe smiled. 'That is very kind of you,' she said. 'But that is not the way to run a business. You will need every pula you can make.'

'If you make any, that is,' muttered Mma Makutsi.

Mma Ramotswe threw a disapproving glance in

67

Mma Makutsi's direction. 'I am sure he will,' she said. 'I am sure of that.'

After Charlie had left the office, Mma Ramotswe fiddled for a moment with a small pile of papers on her desk. She looked across the room at Mma Makutsi, who was studiously avoiding looking at her, and was paging through her shorthand notebook as if it contained some important hidden secret. 'Mma Makutsi,' she said. 'I really need to talk to you.'

Mma Makutsi continued to leaf through the notebook. 'I am here,' she said. 'I am listening, Mma.'

Mma Ramotswe felt her heart beating within her. I am not very good at this sort of thing, she told herself. 'That young man,' she said, 'is just the same as any young man. He has his dreams, as we all did when we were his age. Even you, Mma Makutsi. Even you. You went to the Botswana Secretarial College—you sacrificed so much for that—your people up in Bobonong sacrificed too. You wanted to make something of yourself, and you did.' She paused. Mma Makutsi was sitting quite still, no longer looking through the notebook, which she had laid down on the desk.

'Now everything has turned out well for you,' Mma Ramotswe went on. 'You have your house. You have that fiancé of yours. You will have money when you marry him. But don't forget that there are many others who still don't have what you now have. Don't forget that.'

'I don't see what this has to do with anything,' Mma Makutsi interjected. 'I was merely pointing out what is very clear, Mma. That boy's business will fail because he is no good. Anybody can see

68

that he is no good.'

'No!' said Mma Ramotswe firmly. 'You cannot say that he is no good! You cannot say that.'

'Yes I can,' said Mma Makutsi. 'I can say that because it's the truth, Mma. Your trouble . . .' She paused. 'Your trouble, Mma, is that you're too kind. You let those boys get away with all sorts of things just because you're too kind. Well, I'm a realist. I see things as they really are.'

'Oh,' said Mma Ramotswe. And then she said, again, 'Oh.'

'Yes,' said Mma Makutsi. 'And now, Mma, I shall resign. I do not have to work here and I have decided that it is time to resign. Thank you for everything you have done for me. I hope that you find the filing system is easy to use. You will find everything in the right place when I am gone.'

And with that she rose to her feet and began to walk to the door. She stopped, though, and returned to her desk, where she opened a drawer and began to survey its contents. Mma Ramotswe noticed that she was wearing new shoes: burgundy suede shoes with bows on the toe caps. They were not the shoes of a modest person, she thought. They were . . . and then the description came to her. They were resignation shoes.

CHAPTER SIX

Go in Peace; Stay in Peace

Mr J.L.B. Matekoni had seen crises before. Usually these involved mechanical matters— distraught owners feeling desperate about cars which were needed for some important occasion; the non-arrival of spare parts; the eventual arrival of spare parts, but the wrong ones—there were many ways in which difficult situations could arise in a garage, but he had found that the best response to these was the same in every case. He would sit down and consider the situation carefully. Not only did this help to identify the solution to the problem, but it also gave him the opportunity to remind himself that things were not really as bad as they seemed; it was all a question of perspective. Sitting down and looking up at the sky for a few minutes—not at any particular part of the sky, but just at the sky in general—at the vast, dizzying, empty sky of Botswana, cut human problems down to size. It was not possible to tell what was in that sky, of course, at least during the day; but at night it revealed itself to be an ocean of stars, limitless, white in its infinity; so large, so large, that any of our problems, even the greatest of them, was a small thing. And yet we did not look at it like that, Mr J.L.B. Matekoni thought, and that made us imagine that a blocked fuel feed was a disaster.

He had not wanted Charlie to hand in his resignation, but when the apprentice had asked

70

him about the possibility of using that car as a taxi, he had resisted the temptation to refuse him point-blank. That at least would have solved the problem in the short term. It would have put an end to his immediate plans to start a taxi service, but it would not have scotched the young man's hopes. So he had agreed to the proposition and had watched Charlie's face light up. Mr J.L.B. Matekoni had his reservations about the feasibility of the idea; there was scant profit to be made from taxis unless one over-charged—which some taxi drivers did—or drove too quickly—which all taxi drivers did. Charlie now had his driving licence, but Mr J.L.B. Matekoni had little confidence in his driving ability and had once stopped him and taken over when they were travelling together to pick up a consignment of parts and he had let Charlie take the wheel of the truck.

'We are not in a hurry,' he said. 'Those parts are not going anywhere. And there are no girls to impress.'

The apprentice had sat in the passenger seat, shoulders hunched. He had been silent.

'I'm sorry to have to tell you off,' said Mr J.L.B. Matekoni. 'But that is my job. I have to advise you. That is what an apprentice-master has to do.'

That conversation came back to him now. If he were really serious about his duties, he would have warned Charlie of the folly of not completing his training. He would have spelled out to him the risks of starting one's own business; he would have told him about cash-flow problems and the difficulty of getting credit. Then he would have gone on to warn him about bad debts, which presumably even taxi drivers encountered when

71

people fled the car without paying or when, at the end of a journey, they confessed they did not have quite enough money to pay the fare and would five pula do?

He had done none of this, he reflected; he had said nothing. But his failure, and Charlie's departure, were not the end of the world. If the taxi service did not work, then Charlie could always come back, as he had done the last time he had given up his apprenticeship. That had been when he had gone off with that married woman and had come back, his tail between his legs, when that affair had come to its predictable end. That showed how these young men worked, he thought. They bounced back.

Mma Makutsi's departure, however, was a more serious matter altogether. Mma Makutsi resigned shortly before tea-time, when he and Mr Polopetsi came into the office, their mugs in their hands, expecting to find the tea already brewed. Instead they found Mma Ramotswe sitting at her desk, her head sunk in her hands, while Mma Makutsi was putting the contents of a drawer into a large plastic bag. Mma Makutsi looked up as the men entered the room.

'I have not made tea yet,' she said. 'You will need to put the kettle on yourselves.'

Mr Polopetsi glanced at Mr J.L.B. Matekoni; he stood in some awe of Mma Makutsi, and he was wary of her moods. 'She is a changeable person,' he had explained to his wife. 'She is very clever, but she is changeable. One moment it's this; the next moment, it's that. You have to be very careful.'

Mr J.L.B. Matekoni glanced at Mma Ramotswe, but she, looking up, merely nodded in the direction of the kettle.

Mma Makutsi continued to busy herself with her task of emptying the drawer. 'The reason why I did not put on the kettle is that I have resigned.'

Mr Polopetsi gave a start. 'From making tea?'

'From everything,' snapped Mma Makutsi. 'So I suspect that you will be doing more investigating, Rra, now that I am going. I hope that Mr J.L.B. Matekoni will be able to release you from your duties in the garage.'

The effect on Mr Polopetsi of this remark was immediate. If he had wished to conceal his eagerness to occupy Mma Makutsi's position, then this wish was overcome by his sheer and evident pleasure at the thought of doing more investigative work. And Mma Makutsi, sensing this, decided to take the matter further. 'In fact,' she went on, slamming the drawer shut, 'why don't you take over my desk right now? Here, try this chair. You can put it up a bit by turning this bit here. See. That is for short people like you, Rra.'

Mr Polopetsi put his mug down on Mma Makutsi's desk and moved over to examine the chair. 'That will be fine,' he said. 'I can adjust it. It looks as if it needs a bit of oil, but we have plenty of that in the garage, don't we, Mr J.L.B. Matekoni?'

It was meant to be a joke, and Mr J.L.B. Matekoni smiled weakly, and dutifully. He glanced again at Mma Ramotswe, who was now glaring at her assistant on the other side of the room. It seemed to Mr J.L.B. Matekoni that the most tactful thing to do would be to leave the office and he turned to Mr Polopetsi. 'I think that we should have tea a bit later, Rra,' he said. 'The ladies are busy.'

'But Mma Makutsi . . .' Mr Polopetsi began, but was silenced by a stare from Mr J.L.B. Matekoni, who had already started to move towards the door. Picking up his mug, Mr Polopetsi followed him out of the door and back into the garage.

Mma Ramotswe waited until the door had been closed before she addressed Mma Makutsi. 'I am very sorry,' she said. 'I am very sorry if I have offended you, Mma Makutsi. You know that I have a lot of respect for you. You know that, don't you? I would never deliberately be rude to you. I really would not.'

Mma Makutsi, who had risen to her feet as the two men left, was reaching down for her bag. She straightened up and hesitated for a few moments before she spoke. It seemed as if she was looking for exactly the right words. 'I am aware of that, Mma,' she said slowly. 'I know that. And I am the one who has been rude. But I have made up my mind. I have decided that I am fed up with being number two. I have always been number two, all through my life. I have always been the junior one. Now I am going to be my own boss.' She paused. 'It's not that you are a bad boss. You are a very good one. You are kind. You do not tell me what to do all the time. But I want to be able to speak as I wish. I have never been able to do that—ever. All my life, up in Bobonong, down here, I have been the one who has to watch my tongue and be careful. Now I do not want that any more. Can you understand that, Mma?'

Mma Ramotswe did. 'I can see that. You are a very intelligent woman. You have a piece of paper to prove it.' She pointed to the framed diploma

74

above Mma Makutsi's desk; the words ninety-seven per cent clearly legible even from afar. 'Don't forget to take that, Mma,' she said.

Mma Makutsi looked up at the diploma. 'You could easily have got one of those yourself, Mma,' she said.

'But I didn't,' said Mma Ramotswe. 'You did.'

There was silence for a moment.

'Do you want me to stay?' asked Mma Makutsi. There was an edge of uncertainty in her voice now.

Mma Ramotswe opened her hands in a gesture of acceptance. 'I don't think that you should, Mma,' she said. 'You need a change. I would love you to stay, but I think that you have decided, haven't you, that you need a change.'

'Maybe,' said Mma Makutsi.

'But you will come back and see me, won't you?'

'Of course,' said Mma Makutsi. 'And you will come to my wedding, won't you? You and Mr J.L.B. Matekoni? There will be a seat for you in the front row, Mma Ramotswe. With the aunties.'

There was nothing more to do other than to retrieve the framed diploma from its place on the wall. When it was taken down, there was a white patch where it had been hanging, and they both saw this. Mma Makutsi had been there that long; right from the beginning, really, those humble days in the original office, when chickens came in, uninvited, and pecked at the floor around the desks.

Their words of farewell were polite—the correct ones, as laid down in the old Botswana customs. Tsamaya sentlê: go well. To which the reply was, Sala sentlê: stay well; mere words, of course, but when meant, as now, so powerful. Mma Ramotswe could tell that Mma Makutsi was regretting her decision and did not want to go. It would have been easy to stop this now, to suggest that while Mma Makutsi was replacing the diploma, she, Mma Ramotswe, would start to make the tea. But somehow it seemed too late for that. Sometimes one knew, as Mma Makutsi clearly did, when it was necessary to move on to the next stage of one's life. When this happened, it was not helpful for others to hold one back. So she allowed Mma Makutsi to leave, did nothing to stop her, and it was not until she had been gone for ten minutes or so that Mma Ramotswe began to weep. She wept for the loss of her friend and colleague, but also for everything else that she had lost in this life, and of which, unexpectedly, she was now by a flood of memories reminded: for her father, that great man, Obed Ramotswe, now late; for the child she had known for such a short time, such a precious time; for Seretse Khama, who had been a father to the entire country and who had made it one of the finest places on this earth; for her childhood. She wanted everything back, as we do sometimes in our irrationality and regret; we want it all back.

CHAPTER SEVEN

How Does One Become More Exciting?

If I can fix a car, Mr J.L.B. Matekoni told himself, then I can do a simple thing like find out whether a man is seeing a woman. And yet, now that he came to start the enquiry, he was not sure whether it would be quite as straightforward as he had imagined it would be. He could have asked Mma Ramotswe's advice, but she was preoccupied with the consequences of Mma Makutsi's departure and he did not want to add to her burdens. As far as the garage was concerned, Charlie still had to work a week's notice—he had spared him a longer period than that, although he would have been entitled to insist on a month. Fortunately since it was a relatively quiet period—the school holidays, when people tended not to find fault with their cars and when thoughts of routine servicing were put aside—it would be easy for Mr J.L.B. Matekoni to take a few hours off every day, should the need arise. The younger apprentice was slightly more reliable than Charlie, anyway, and could now cope with many routine garage tasks, and Mr Polopetsi was also showing himself to be a natural mechanic. Of course he had aspirations to Mma Makutsi's job, but Mr J.L.B. Matekoni doubted whether these ambitions would be satisfied. Mma Makutsi had done a lot of filing and typing, and he could not see Mr Polopetsi settling down to these mundane tasks. He wanted to be out and about, looking into things, and what Mma Ramotswe had said about his talents in this respect suggested that she might not be keen for him to do too much of that.

It was all very well being confident, but as you climbed the outside staircase of the President Hotel, on your way to meet the client for your first proper conversation with her, then you felt a certain anxiety. It was not dissimilar to the way you felt when, as an apprentice, you stripped an engine down by yourself for the very first time, decoked it and fitted new piston rings. Would everything fit together again? Would it work? He looked over his shoulder at the scene in the square below. Traders had set up stalls, no more than upturned boxes in many cases, or rugs laid out on the concrete paving, and were selling their wares to passers-by: combs, hair preparations, trinkets, carvings for visitors. In one corner, a small knot of people clustered around a seller of traditional medicines, listening carefully as the gnarled herbalist explained to them the merits of the barks and roots that he had ranged in front of him. He at least knew what he was talking about, thought Mr J.L.B. Matekoni; he at least was doing what he had always done, and doing it well, unlike those who suddenly decide, in mid-life, that they want to become private detectives . . .

He reached the top of the stairway and entered under the cool canopies of the hotel's verandah. He looked about him; only a few of the tables were occupied, and he saw Mma Botumile immediately, sitting at the far end, a cup of coffee before her. He stood still for a moment and took a deep breath. She looked up and saw him and gestured to the empty chair at her table.

'I have been waiting, Rra,' she said, looking at her watch. 'You said . . .'

Mr J.L.B. Matekoni consulted his own watch. He had made a point of being on time and had not expected to be censured for lateness. She had said eleven o'clock, had she not? He felt a pang of doubt.

'Ten forty-five,' she said. 'You said ten forty-five.'

He was flustered. 'I thought I said eleven. I am

sorry, Mma. I thought . . .'

She brushed aside his apology. 'It does not matter,' she said. 'Where is Mma Ramotswe?'

'She is in the office,' he said. 'She has assigned me to this case.'

Mma Botumile, who had been lifting her cup of coffee to her lips, put it down sharply. A small splash of coffee spilled over the rim of the cup and fell on the table. 'Why is she not dealing with this?' she asked coldly. 'Does she think that I am not important enough for her? Is that it? Well, there are other detectives, I'll have you know.'

'There aren't,' said Mr J.L.B. Matekoni politely. 'The No. 1 Ladies' Detective Agency is the only agency. There are no other detectives that I know of.'

Mma Botumile digested this information. She looked Mr J.L.B. Matekoni up and down before she spoke again. 'I thought that you were the mechanic.'

'I am,' he said. 'But I also do investigations.' He thought for a few moments. 'It is useful to have an ordinary occupation while at the same time you conduct enquiries.' He had no idea why this should be so, but it seemed to him to be a reasonable thing to say.

Mma Botumile lifted up her coffee cup again. 'Do you know my husband?' she asked.

Mr J.L.B. Matekoni shook his head. 'You must tell me about him,' he said. 'That is why I wanted to meet you today. I need to know something more about him before I can find out what he is doing.'

A waitress came to the table and looked expectantly at Mr J.L.B. Matekoni. He had not thought about what he would have, but now he felt that tea would be the right thing on a morning like this, which was getting hotter—you could feel it. He was about to order when Mma Botumile waved the waitress away. 'We don't need anything,' she said.

He watched in astonishment as the waitress walked off. 'I thought that I . . .' he began.

'No time,' said Mma Botumile. 'This is business, remember. I am paying for your time, I take it. Two hundred pula an hour, or something like that?'

Mr J.L.B. Matekoni did not know what to say. There would be a fee, of course, but he had not thought about what it would be. He was accustomed to charging for mechanical work and he imagined that each case would have its mechanical equivalent. Finding out about an errant husband would be the equivalent perhaps of a full service, with oil change and attention to brakes. A more complex enquiry might be charged at the same rate as the replacement of a timing chain. He had not worked any of this out, but he would certainly not be charging two hundred pula an hour to sit and talk on the verandah of the President Hotel.

Mr J.L.B. Matekoni was a tolerant man, not given to animosity of any sort, but as he gazed at Mma Botumile he found himself developing a strong dislike for her. But he knew, too, that this was dangerous; he knew that as a professional person he should keep personal feelings strictly out of the picture. He had heard Mma Ramotswe talk about this before, and he had agreed with her. One simply could not allow one's feelings to get in the way of one's judgement. It was exactly the same with cars: emotion should not come into decisions about a car's future, no matter what the bonds between the car and the owner. But then there was Mma Ramotswe's tiny white van; if ever there were a case for not allowing emotion to cloud one's view of a vehicle, then that was it. He had nursed and cajoled that vehicle when good sense suggested that it should be replaced by something more modern, but Mma Ramotswe would have none of that. 'I cannot see myself in a new car,' she said. 'I am a tiny white van person. That is what I want.'

He lowered his gaze; Mma Botumile was staring back at him and he felt uncomfortable. 'You must tell me about your husband,' he said. 'I must know the sort of things that he likes to do.'

Mma Botumile settled back in her chair. 'My husband is not a very strong man,' she said. 'He is one of those men who does not really know what he wants. I can tell, of course, what he wants, but he cannot.' She looked at Mr J.L.B. Matekoni as if expecting a challenge to this, but when none came she continued. 'We have been married for twenty years now, which is a long time. We met when we were both students at the University of Botswana. I am a B.Com. you see. He is an accountant with a mining company.

'We built a house out over near the Western by-pass, near where the Grand Palm Hotel is. It is a very fine house—you may have seen it from the road, Rra. It has gates which go like this—large gates. You know the place?'

Mr J.L.B. Matekoni did, and he had often wondered who would build gates like those; now he knew.

81

He nodded and waited for her to continue, but she was silent, watching him over the rim of her coffee cup.

'And was this marriage a happy one?' he asked finally. He found that the question came out in those words without his really having to think very much about it. Where had it come from? He suddenly remembered: years before, he had been in the High Court in Lobatse, waiting to give evidence in a case involving a road accident, and he had slipped into one of the courts to watch a case. He remembered the lawyer standing at his table, facing a woman who was sitting in the witness box, crying. And the lawyer suddenly spoke and said to her: 'And was this marriage a happy one?' and the woman had started to cry all the more. What a ridiculous question, he had thought; what a ridiculous question to ask of a woman who was in floods of tears. Of course the marriage was not a happy one. But the question itself had sounded so impressive, that he had remembered it, little thinking that years later he would be able to use those precise words.

Unlike the witness, Mma Botumile did not burst into tears. 'Of course it was happy,' she said. 'And still is. Or rather, could be, if he stopped seeing that other woman.'

'Have you spoken to him about her?' Mr J.L.B. Matekoni asked.

Mma Botumile was dismissive. 'Of course not! And, anyway, what could I say? I know nothing about this woman, whoever she is. That is for you to find out.'

Mr J.L.B. Matekoni pondered this for a moment. 'But you do know that he's seeing a woman, do you?' he asked.

'Oh, I know that all right,' said Mma Botumile. 'Women know these things.'

Intuition, thought Mr J.L.B. Matekoni. That's what women claimed they had and men did not, or did not have enough of: intuition. He had often wondered, though, how one could know something without actually hearing it, or seeing it, or even smelling it. If one did not acquire knowledge from one's senses, then where would one acquire it? That's what he would have liked to ask Mma Botumile, but felt that he could not. She was not a woman, he felt, who would take well to being challenged.

'I see,' he said mildly. 'But, do you mind telling me how women know these things? I'm sure they do know them, but how come?'

For the first time in the course of their meeting, Mma Botumile smiled. 'It's easier to talk to another woman about these matters,' she said. 'But since your Mma Ramotswe is so busy I suppose that I shall have to talk to you, Rra.'

Mr J.L.B. Matekoni waited.

Mma Botumile lowered her voice. 'Men make certain demands of ladies,' she said. 'And if they stop, then it's a very good sign. Any woman knows that.'

Mr J.L.B. Matekoni caught his breath.

There was a glint of amusement in Mma Botumile's eye. 'Yes,' she said. 'That is always a sign that the man has another friend.'

Mr J.L.B. Matekoni did not know what to say. He looked down at the table, and then at the floor. Somebody had spilled some sugar from the table, a small line of white grains, and he noticed that a troop of ants, marshalled with military precision, had arrived to carry them off, minuscule porters staggering under the weight of their trophies.

'So that is what you need to find out, Rra,' said Mma Botumile, signalling to the waitress to bring her bill. 'You will have to follow him and find out who this lady is. I can give you no help about that—that is why I have asked you. That is why you are being paid two hundred pula an hour.'

'I'm not,' muttered Mr J.L.B. Matekoni.

*　　　*　　　*

He left the President Hotel uncertain what to do and unsure, he now realised, whether he wanted to carry out this investigation at all. The meeting with Mma Botumile had not been a satisfactory one. She had given him no guidance as to where he might start looking for her husband's girlfriend, and the only suggestion that she had made was that Mr J.L.B. Matekoni might follow him after work one day and see where he went. 'He certainly doesn't come home straightaway,' she said. 'He says that he's seeing clients, but I don't believe that, do you?' Mr J.L.B. Matekoni muttered something which could have been yes or equally could have been no. He did not like being expected to take sides like this, and yet, he told himself, this is what must be expected of people like private detectives, or lawyers, for that matter. People paid them to take their side, and this meant that you had to believe in what the client wanted. The thought made him feel very uncomfortable. What if you were to be hired by somebody whom you could not bear, or if you found out that the person

84

who had engaged you was lying? Would you have to pretend that you believed the lies—which would be impossible, thought Mr J.L.B. Matekoni—or could you tell them that you would have no truck with their falsehoods?

And then another thought struck Mr J.L.B. Matekoni as he made his way down the steps of the President Hotel. He had never met Mma Botumile's husband and he had no idea what he was like. But it occurred to him, nonetheless, that when he eventually met him—if he eventually met him—he would probably feel sorry for him and end up rather liking him. If he were to be married to Mma Botumile, who he considered both rude and bossy, then would he not himself seek comfort elsewhere, in the arms of a good, sympathetic woman—somebody like Mma Ramotswe in fact? Of course Mma Ramotswe would never look at another man—Mr J.L.B. Matekoni knew that. He stopped. It had never once crossed his mind that Mma Ramotswe might take up with somebody else, but then many people who were let down in this way by their spouses never thought that this would happen to them, and yet it did. So there were many people who deluded themselves.

It was a very unwelcome thought, and Mr J.L.B. Matekoni felt himself becoming hot and uncomfortable as he stood there in front of the President Hotel, thinking the unthinkable. He saw himself coming home one evening and discovering a man's tie, perhaps, draped over a chair. He saw himself picking up the tie, examining it, and then dangling it in front of Mma Ramotswe and saying, *How could you, Mma Ramotswe? How could you?* And she would look anywhere but in his eyes and say, *Well, Mr J.L.B. Matekoni, it's not as if you have been a very exciting husband, you know*. It was ridiculous. Mma Ramotswe would never say a thing like that; he had done his best to be a good husband to her. He had never strayed, and he had helped around the house as modern husbands are meant to do. In fact, he had done everything in his power to be modern, even when that had not been particularly easy.

Suddenly Mr J.L.B. Matekoni felt unaccountably sad. A man might try to be modern—and succeed, to a degree—but it was very difficult to be exciting. Women these days had magazines which showed them exciting men—bright-eyed men, posed with smiling women, and everyone clearly enjoying themselves greatly. The men would perhaps be holding a car key, or even be leaning against an expensive German vehicle, and the women would be laughing at something that the exciting men had said, something exciting. Surely Mma Ramotswe would not be influenced by such artificiality, and yet she certainly did look at these magazines, which were passed on to her by Mma Makutsi. She affected to laugh at them, but then if she really found them so ridiculous, surely she would not bother to read them in the first place?

Mr J.L.B. Matekoni stood at the edge of the square, looking over the traders' stalls, deep in thought. Then he asked himself a question which, although easily posed, was rather more difficult to answer: how does a husband become more exciting?

CHAPTER EIGHT

An Account of a Puzzling Conversation

That evening, Mr J.L.B. Matekoni made his way to the address which Mma Botumile had given him as they had sat on the verandah of the President Hotel; sat tealess, in his case, because she had so selfishly dismissed the waitress. It was a modest office block, three storeys high, on Kudumatse Drive, flanked on either side by equally undistinguished buildings, a furniture warehouse and a workshop that repaired electric fans. He parked his truck on the opposite side of the road, in a position where he could see the front entrance to the offices, but sufficiently far away so as not to look suspicious to anybody who should emerge from the building. He was just a man in a truck; the sort of man, and the sort of truck, one saw all the time on the roads of Gaborone; quite unexceptional. Most of those men, and trucks, were busy going somewhere, but occasionally they stopped, as this man had done, and waited for something or other to happen. It was not an unusual sight.

Mr J.L.B. Matekoni looked at his watch. It was now almost five o'clock, the time when, according to Mma Botumile, her husband invariably left the office. He was a creature of habit, she said, even if some of these habits had become bad ones. If Mr J.L.B. Matekoni were to wait outside the office, he would see him coming out and getting into his large red car, which would be parked by the side of

87

the building. There was no need to give a detailed description of him, she said, as he could be identified by his car.

'What make of car is it?' Mr J.L.B. Matekoni had asked politely. He would never describe a car simply by its colour, and it astonished him that people did this. He had noticed Mma Makutsi doing it, and even Mma Ramotswe, who should have known better, described cars in terms of their colour, without making any reference to make or engine capacity.

Mma Botumile had looked at him almost with pity. 'How do you expect me to know that?' she said. 'You're the mechanic.'

He had bitten his lip at the rudeness of the response. It was unusual in Botswana, a polite country, to come across such behaviour, and when one did encounter it, it appeared all the more surprising, and unpleasant. He was at a loss as to why she should be so curt in her manner. In his experience bad behaviour came from those who were unsure of themselves, those who had some obscure point to make. Mma Botumile was a woman of position, a successful woman who had nothing to prove to anybody; certainly she had no reason to belittle Mr J.L.B. Matekoni, who could hardly have been any threat to her. So, why should she be so rude? Did she dislike all men, or just him; and if it was just him, then what was there about him that so offended her?

Now, sitting in the cab of his truck, he looked over the road towards the side of the building where, he suddenly noticed, two large red cars were parked. For a moment he felt despair—this whole thing had been a mistake from the very outset—but then he thought: the odds were surely against there being two drivers of red cars who would leave the building at exactly five o'clock. Of course not: the first man to come out after five o'clock would be Mma Botumile's husband.

He consulted his watch again. It was one minute to five now, and at any moment Rra Botumile might walk out of the front door. He looked up from his watch, and at that moment two men emerged from the office building, deep in conversation with one another; two men in white shirtsleeves and ties, jackets slung over their shoulders, the very picture of the office-worker at the end of the day. Mr J.L.B. Matekoni watched them as they turned the corner of the building and approached the cars, lingered for a moment to conclude their conversation, and then each got into a red car.

For a few moments, Mr J.L.B. Matekoni sat quite still. He had no way of telling which of the two men was Mma Botumile's husband, which meant that either he would have to give up and go home, or he would have to make a very quick decision and follow one of them. It would be easy enough to drive off and abandon the enquiry, but that would involve going back to Mma Ramotswe and telling her that he had failed at his attempt at doing what he understood to be the simplest and most basic of the procedures of her profession. He had not read Clovis Andersen's *The Principles of Private Detection*, of course, and he wondered whether Mma Ramotswe's trusted *vade mecum* would give any instruction on what to do in circumstances like this. Presumably he would point out that you must at least have a description of the

89

person you are interested in at the outset, which of course he had not obtained.

Mr J.L.B. Matekoni made a snap decision. He would follow the first car as it came out. There were no grounds for thinking that this was Mr Botumile, but he had to choose, and he might as well . . . Or should he go for the second? There was something about the second which *looked* suspicious. The driver of the first car was obviously acting confidently and decisively in leaving first. That showed a clear conscience, whereas the second driver, contemplating the dissemblance and the tryst that lay ahead, showed the hesitation of one with a guilty conscience. It was a slender straw of surmise, but one which Mr J.L.B. Matekoni grasped at in the absence of anything better. That would impress Clovis Andersen—and Mma Ramotswe—he thought: a decision based on a sound understanding of human psychology—and from a garage mechanic too!

The snap decision, so confident and decisive, was reversed, and Mr J.L.B. Matekoni waited while the first of the two red cars swung out into the main road and drove off. At five o'clock on this road there was a fair bit of traffic to contend with, as people, anxious to return home, drove off to Gaborone West and onto the Lobatse Road, and to other places they lived; all of them going about their legitimate business, of course, unlike the second driver, who seemed to be hesitating. He had started his engine—a mechanic could tell that at a glance, even from that distance—but he was not moving for some reason. Mr J.L.B. Matekoni wondered why he should be waiting, and decided that this was a yet further indication of guilt: he

90

was waiting until the driver of the other red car was well on his way, as he did not want that first driver to see him, the second driver, setting off in the wrong direction. That was clearly what was happening. Again, Mr J.L.B. Matekoni was astonished at the way in which these conclusions came to mind. It seemed to him that once one started to think about a problem like this, everything all fitted into place surprisingly neatly, like one of those puzzles one saw in the papers where all the numbers added up or the missing letters made sense. He had not tried his hand at those, but perhaps he should. He had read somewhere that if you used your mind like that, then you kept it in good order for a longer period of time, and you put off the day when you would be sitting in the sun, like some of the very old people, not exactly sure which day of the week it was and wondering why the world no longer made the sense that it once did. Yet such people were often happy, he reminded himself, possibly because it did not really matter what day of the week it was anyway. And if they remembered nothing of the recent past but still held on to memories of twenty years ago, then that, too, might not be as bad as people might think. For many of us, thought Mr J.L.B. Matekoni, twenty years ago was a rather nice time. The world slipped away from us as we got older— of course it did—but perhaps we should not hold on too tightly.

The red car ahead of Mr J.L.B. Matekoni went up Kudumatse Drive and continued on the road that led out to Kanye. The buildings became smaller—offices and small warehouses became houses; dirt roads went off on both sides to newly built dwellings, two-bedroomed embodiments of somebody's ambitions, dreams, hard work, carved out of what had not all that long ago been thorn bush, grazing for cattle. He saw a car he thought he recognised, parked outside one of these; a car that he had worked on only a few weeks ago. It belonged to a teacher at Gaborone Secondary School, a man who everybody said would one day be a headmaster. His wife went to the Anglican Cathedral on Sunday mornings, Mma Ramotswe reported, and sang all the hymns lustily, although quite out of tune. 'But she is doing her best,' added Mma Ramotswe.

Suddenly the red car slowed down. Mr J.L.B. Matekoni had been keeping his truck three vehicles behind it, as he did not want to be spotted by Mr Botumile, and now he was faced with a decision as to whether he should pull in—which surely would look suspicious—or overtake. Two cars ahead of him started to overtake, but Mr J.L.B. Matekoni did not follow them. Steering over to the side of the road, he watched what was happening ahead. The red car started to move more quickly, and then, with very little warning, swung round onto the other side of the road and headed back in the direction from which it had come. Mr J.L.B. Matekoni continued on his course. He had a glimpse of the driver of the red car—just a face, staring fixedly ahead, not enough to remember, or to judge—and then all he saw was the rear of the car heading back towards town. He looked in his driving mirror—the road was clear, and he turned, going some way off the edge of the tar, as his truck had a wide turning circle.

Fortunately the traffic returning to town was

lighter, and Mr J.L.B. Matekoni soon found himself closing on Mr Botumile's car. He slowed down, but not too much, as this was an unpredictable quarry, like a wild animal in the bush that will suddenly turn and dart off in an unexpected direction to elude capture. Ahead of him the rays of the sinking sun had caught the windows of the Government buildings off Khama Crescent and were flashing signals. Red. Stop, Mr J.L.B. Matekoni. Stop. Go back to what you understand.

Mr Botumile drove through the centre of town, past the Princess Marina Hospital, and on towards the Gaborone Sun Hotel. Then he stopped, parking in front of the hotel just as Mr J.L.B. Matekoni turned his truck into a different section of the hotel parking lot and turned off the engine. Then both men left their vehicles and entered the hotel, Mr Botumile going first, alone—he thought—and Mr J.L.B. Matekoni following him a discreet distance behind, his heart beating hard within him at the sheer excitement of what he was doing. This is better, he thought, infinitely better than adjusting brake pads and replacing oil filters.

* * *

'Mr Gotso?' exclaimed Mma Ramotswe. 'Mr Charlie Gotso? Him?'

'Yes,' said Mr J.L.B. Matekoni. 'I recognised him immediately—who wouldn't? Charlie Gotso was sitting there and when I saw him I had to look away quickly. Not that he would know who I am. He'd know who you are, Mma Ramotswe. You've spoken to him, haven't you? All those years ago

93

when . . .'

'That was a long time ago,' Mma Ramotswe said. 'And I was just a small person to him. Men like that don't remember small people.'

'You are not small, Mma,' Mr J.L.B. Matekoni found himself protesting, but stopped. Mma Ramotswe was not small.

She looked at him with amusement. 'No, I am not small, Rra. You are right. But I was thinking of how I would mean nothing to a man like that.'

Mr J.L.B. Matekoni was quick to assent. 'Of course that's what you meant. I know men like that. They are very arrogant.'

'He is a rich man,' said Mma Ramotswe. 'Rich men sometimes forget that they are people, just like the rest of us.' She paused. 'So there was Charlie Gotso, no less! And Mr Botumile went straight up to him and sat down?'

Mr J.L.B. Matekoni nodded. He and Mma Ramotswe were sitting at the kitchen table in their house on Zebra Drive. Behind them, on the stove, a pan of chopped pumpkin was on the boil, filling the air with that familiar chalky smell of the yellow pumpkin flesh. Inside the oven, a small leg of lamb was slowly roasting; it would be a good meal, when it was eventually served in half an hour or so. There was time enough, then, to talk, and for Mr J.L.B. Matekoni to give Mma Ramotswe an account of the enquiry from which he had just returned.

'This was outside,' he said. 'You know that bar at the back? That place. And since there were quite a few people there, and most of the tables were occupied, I was able to sit down at the table next to theirs without it appearing odd.'

'You did the right thing,' said Mma Ramotswe. Clovis Andersen, in *The Principles of Private Detection*, advised that it could look just as odd to distance oneself unnaturally from the object of one's attention as to come too close. *Neither too near nor too far*, he wrote. *That's what the Ancients called the golden mean, and they were right—as always!* She had wondered who these ancients were; whether they were the same people whom one called the elders in Botswana, or whether they were somebody else altogether. But the important thing was that Mr J.L.B. Matekoni, who had never read *The Principles of Private Detection*, should have done just the right thing without any specialist knowledge. This only went to show, she decided, that much of what was written in *The Principles of Private Detection* was simply common sense, leading to decisions at which one could have anyway arrived unaided.

Mr J.L.B. Matekoni accepted the compliment graciously. 'Thank you, Mma. Well, there I was sitting at the table, so close to Charlie Gotso that I could see the place on his neck where he has a barber's rash—rough skin, Mma, like a little ploughed field. And there were flecks on his collar from the blood.'

Mma Ramotswe made a face. 'Poor man.'

Mr J.L.B. Matekoni looked at her in surprise. 'He is no good, that man.'

'Of course not,' Mma Ramotswe corrected herself. 'But I would not wish anybody to be uncomfortable, would you, Mr J.L.B. Matekoni?'

He thought for a moment, and then agreed. He did not wish misfortune on anybody, he decided, even if they deserved it. Mma Ramotswe was undoubtedly right about that, even if she was inclined to be a little bit too generous in her judgements.

'They started to talk, and I pretended to be very interested in reading the menu which the waiter had brought me.' He laughed. 'I read about the price of a Castle lager and about the various sorts of sandwich fillings. Then I read it all again.

'In the meantime, I was listening as closely as I could to what they were saying. It was a bit hard, as there was somebody sitting nearby who was laughing like a donkey. But I did hear something.'

Mma Ramotswe frowned. 'Excuse me, Mr J.L.B. Matekoni,' she said. 'But why were you listening to them? Where was the woman?'

'What woman?' asked Mr J.L.B. Matekoni.

'The woman with whom Mr Botumile is having an affair,' Mma Ramotswe replied. 'That woman.'

Mr J.L.B. Matekoni looked up at the ceiling. He had expected to see Mr Botumile meeting a woman, and when he had sat down next to Charlie Gotso he thought that perhaps the woman would arrive a bit later; that they both knew Mr Gotso. But then, even when it became apparent that no woman would be joining them, he found himself engrossed in the encounter that was taking place at the neighbouring table. This was more interesting than mere adultery; this was the edge of something much more important than that. He imagined now that he would be able to reveal to Mma Botumile that her husband was up to something far worse than that which she had imagined; he was consorting with no less a person than Charlie Gotso, the least salubrious of Gaborone's businessmen, a man who used intimidation and fear as instruments of persuasion; a bad man, in fact, to put it simply. And Mr J.L.B. Matekoni had no reluctance to use unadorned, direct language, whether about cars, or people. Just as there were some bad cars—cars that were consistently slow to start or that invariably had inexplicable, incorrigible rattles—so too there were bad people. Fortunately there were not too many of these in Botswana, but there were some, and Mr Charlie Gotso was certainly one of them.

'There was no sign of that woman,' he conceded. 'Maybe it was not his evening for seeing her. There will be time enough to find her.'

'I see,' said Mma Ramotswe. 'All right. But what did they talk about anyway?'

'Mining,' said Mr J.L.B. Matekoni. 'Mr Botumile said something about bad results. He said that the cores had come in and that the results were not good.'

Mma Ramotswe shrugged. 'Prospecting,' she said. 'People do that all the time.'

'Then he said: the share price will come down in two weeks, in Johannesburg. And Mr Gotso asked him if he was sure about that. And he replied yes he was.'

'And then?' prompted Mma Ramotswe.

'Then Mr Gotso said that he was very pleased.'

Mma Ramotswe was puzzled. 'Pleased? Why would he be pleased about bad news?'

Mr J.L.B. Matekoni thought for a moment. 'Perhaps it's because he is such an unpleasant man,' he said. 'Perhaps he likes to hear of the misfortune of others. There are people like that.'

Yes, thought Mma Ramotswe. There were such people, but she did not think that Charlie Gotso was like that. He was the sort of person who would be unmoved by the misfortune of others; completely uninterested. All that he would be pleased about would be those things that were in his interests, that made him richer, and this raised a very difficult question: why should the failure of prospectors to find minerals be good news for a bad man?

They finished their conversation on that note. Mr J.L.B. Matekoni had nothing further to report, and the pumpkin and the lamb, judging from the smell from the pot and from the oven, were both ready, or just about. It was time for dinner.

CHAPTER NINE

The Understanding of Shoes

Mma Makutsi awoke the next morning slightly earlier than normal. It had been another cold night, and her room, which had no heating apart from a one-bar electric heater—which was turned off—was still chilly. When the sun came up properly, the light would flood in through her window and warm the place up, but that would not happen for twenty minutes or so. She looked at her watch. If she got up now, she would have fifteen minutes or so in hand before she went off to catch her minibus into work. She could use this time to do something constructive, some sewing, perhaps, on the new sewing machine which Phuti Radiphuti had bought her. She was making a dress for herself and had all the panels cut out, pinned together, and ready for the machine. Now all she needed was a bit of time. She could do fifteen minutes of work on it that morning and then, when she came home from work, she could devote at least two hours to the task, which might well be enough to finish it off.

But there would be no going to work that day, and now that she remembered this she opened her eyes wide, astonished by the realisation. I do not have to get up, she said to herself. I can stay in bed. She closed her eyes again, and nestled her head back into her pillow; but she could not keep her eyes closed, she could not drift back to sleep, for she was wide awake. On a cold morning an extra few minutes of sleep, snatched in denial of the imminent call of the alarm clock, would normally be irresistible. But not now; that which we have, we suddenly find we do not want. She sat up in bed, shivered, and tentatively lowered her feet onto the cement floor of her room. There might be running water in the house, and electric light, but in the villages and in the country they still had floors, here and there, which did not freeze your feet like this—floors made of the dung of cattle, sweet-smelling dung, packed down hard and mixed with mud to give a surface that was cool in the heat and warm to the touch in the cold weather. For all that modern buildings were more comfortable, there were some things, some traditional things, that could not be improved upon.

This thought of things traditional reminded her of Mma Ramotswe, and with a sudden jolt of regret she realised that she would not be seeing her former employer today. A day—a weekday too—with no Mma Ramotswe; it seemed strange,

99

almost ominous, like a day on which something dark was due to happen. But she put that thought out of her mind. She had resigned and had moved on. That's what people said these days—they talked about moving on. Well, that's what she had done, and presumably people who moved on did not look back. So she would not cast an eye back to her old life as an assistant detective; she would look forward to her new life as Mrs Phuti Radiphuti, wife of the proprietor of the Double Comfort Furniture Store, *former* secretary.

It was strange having breakfast and not having to rush; strange eating toast without glancing at the clock; and strange, too, not having to leave the second cup of tea half-finished simply because time had run out. Breakfast that morning seemed not to finish—it merely petered out. The last crumbs of toast were cleared from the plate, the last sip of tea taken, and then . . . nothing. Mma Makutsi sat at her table and thought of the day ahead. There was the dress—she could easily finish that this morning, but somehow she did not want to. She was enjoying the making of that garment, and she had no material for another one. If she finished the dress, then there would be one less thing to do, and her new sewing machine would have to go back into the cupboard. She could clean the house, of course; there was always something to attend to in a house, no matter how regularly one swept and scrubbed. But although she kept the house spick and span, that was not a task that she actually enjoyed, and she had spent almost the entire last weekend giving it a thorough cleaning.

She looked about the room. Her living room, where she ate her breakfast, was sparsely furnished. There was the table at which she now sat—a table condemned by Phuti Radiphuti who had promised to replace it, but had not yet done so; there was a small second-hand settee that she had bought through a newspaper advertisement and which now sported the satin-covered cushions which Phuti Radiphuti had given her; there was a side table on which she had placed several small framed pictures of her family in Bobonong. And that, apart from a small red rug, was it.

She could do something more about decorating the room, she thought. But then if she was going to get married in January, when she would move to Phuti Radiphuti's house, there seemed little point in doing much to her own place. The landlord would be pleased, no doubt, if she went to the hardware store and bought some paint for the walls, but again there seemed to be no point in doing that. Indeed, there seemed to be little point in doing anything.

No sooner had she reached that conclusion, than she realised how absurd it was. Of course there was a point in doing something. Mma Makutsi was not one to waste her time, and she now told herself that her resignation should be a challenge to her to work out a new routine of activity. Yes, she would take advantage of this and do something fresh, something exciting with her life. She would . . . She thought. There must be something. She could get a new job, perhaps. She had read about a new employment agency which had opened which would specialise, it had been announced, in the placing of high-class secretaries. 'This agency is not for everyone,' the press announcement had read. 'We are for the cream of the crop. We are for people who go the extra mile—every day.'

Mma Makutsi had seen the advertisement in the *Botswana Daily News* and had been struck by the wording. She liked the expression *go the extra mile*, which had the ring of a journey to it; and that, she thought, was what life really was—it was a journey. In her case, the journey had started in Bobonong, and had been by bus, all the way down to Gaborone. And then it had become a metaphorical journey, not a real one, but a journey nonetheless. There had been the journey to her final grade at the Botswana Secretarial College, with the marks as milestones along the way: sixty- eight per cent in her first examination, seventy-four in the second; then on to eighty-five per cent; and finally, in a seemingly impossible leap, ninety-seven per cent, and the glory that had come with that. That had surely been a journey.

And then there had come the hunt for the first job—a journey of disappointing blind alleys and wrong turnings, as she discovered that at that level of secretarial employment a crude form of discrimination was at work. She had gone to interview after interview, dressed in the sole good dress that she possessed, and had discovered time and time again that the employer was not in the slightest bit interested in how she had done at the College. All that was required was that one should have passed and got the diploma; that was all. What was on the diploma did not matter, it seemed; all that counted was that one should be glamorous, which Mma Makutsi was realistic enough to know she was not. She had those large round glasses; she had that difficult skin; her clothes spoke of the hardship of her life. No, she was not glamorous.

Here was an agency, though, that implied that hard work and persistence would be rewarded. And the reward would come, no doubt, in the shape of a challenging and interesting job, with a large company, she imagined, in an office with air conditioning and a gleaming staff canteen. She would move amongst highly motivated people, who would be smartly dressed. She would live in a world of memos and targets and workshops. It would be a world away from the No. 1 Ladies' Detective Agency, with its battered old filing cabinets and its two tea-pots.

She had made up her mind, and the decision made her feel more optimistic about the day ahead. She rose from the table and began to wash up the breakfast plates. Two hours later, having made satisfactory progress with her new dress, she put away the sewing machine, locked the house, and began to walk into town. It was a cool day, but the sun was still there; it was perfect, she thought; it was weather for walking, and for thinking as one walked. The doubts of the earlier part of the day had disappeared and now seemed so baseless, so unimportant. She would miss Mma Ramotswe, just as she would miss any friend, but to think, as she did, that her life would be empty without her was a piece of nonsense. There would be plenty of new colleagues once she started her new job and, without being disloyal to Mma Ramotswe, many of them would perhaps be a little bit more exciting than her former employer. It was all very well being of traditional shape, believing in the old Botswana values, and drinking bush tea, but there was another world to explore, a world filled with exciting, modern people, the people who formed opinions, who set the pace in fashion and in witty things to say. That was the world to which she could now graduate, although of course she would always have a soft spot for Mma Ramotswe and the No. 1 Ladies' Detective Agency. Even a thoroughly modern person would like Mma Ramotswe, in the way in which modern people can retain affection for their aunts back in the villages even though they really had nothing in common any more with those aunts.

She had kept the issue of the paper in which the advertisement appeared, and had noted down the address of the agency. It was not a long way away—a half hour walk at the most—and this walk went quickly, made all the quicker by the thoughts she was entertaining of the interview that no doubt lay ahead of her.

'Ninety-seven per cent?' the agency person might say. 'Is that correct? Not a misprint?'

'No, Mma. Ninety-seven per cent.'

'Well, that's very impressive, I must say! And there's a job which I think would be just right for you. It's a pretty high-level job, mind you. But then you've been . . .'

'An associate detective. Second from the top in the organisation.'

'I see. Well, I think you're the lady for the job. The pay is good, by the way. And all the usual benefits.'

'Air conditioning?'

'Naturally.'

The thought of this exchange was deeply satisfying; absorbing, too, with the result that she walked past her destination and had to turn back and retrace her footsteps. But there it was, the Superior Positions Office Employment Agency, on the second floor of a slightly run-down, but still promising-looking building not far from the Catholic church. Once she had climbed the stairs, she saw a sign pointing down a corridor inviting visitors to ring the bell on the door and enter. The corridor was dark, and had a slightly unpleasant smell to it, but the door of the agency office had been recently painted and, reflected Mma Makutsi, she was not going to work there, in that building, which was only a means to a much better-appointed end.

It was a small room, dominated by a desk in the middle of the floor. At this desk there was a slight young woman with elaborately braided hair. She was applying varnish to her nails as Mma Makutsi entered, and she looked up with a vague air of annoyance that she should be disturbed in this task. But she greeted Mma Makutsi in the proper way before asking, 'Do you have an appointment, Mma?'

Mma Makutsi shook her head. 'Your advertisement in the *Daily News* said that none was necessary.'

The receptionist pursed her lips. 'You should not believe everything you read in the papers, Mma,' she said. 'I don't.'

'Even when it's your own advertisement?' asked Mma Makutsi.

For a moment the receptionist said nothing. She dipped the varnish brush into the container and dabbed it thoughtfully on the nail of an index finger.

'You're an experienced secretary, Mma?' she

asked at last.

'Yes,' said Mma Makutsi. 'And I'd like to see somebody more senior, please.'

A further silence ensued. Then the receptionist picked up her telephone and spoke into the receiver.

'She'll see you in a few minutes, Mma,' she said. 'She's seeing somebody else at the moment. You can wait over there.' She pointed to a chair in the corner of the room. Beside the chair was a small table laden with magazines.

Mma Makutsi sat down. She had encountered rude receptionists before and she wondered what it was about the job that seemed sometimes to attract unfriendly people. Perhaps it was that people did the opposite of what they really wanted to do. There were gentle prison guards and soldiers; there were unkind nurses; there were ignorant and unhelpful teachers. And then there were those unfriendly receptionists.

She did not have to wait long. After a few minutes the door to the inner office opened and a young woman walked out. She was carrying a folded piece of paper and was smiling. She walked over to the receptionist and whispered something into her ear. There was laughter.

When the young woman had left, the receptionist glanced at the door and gestured for Mma Makutsi to go in. Then she continued with her nail-painting. Mma Makutsi rose to her feet and made her way to the door, knocked, and without waiting for an invitation, went in.

*　　　*　　　*

They looked at one another in astonishment. Mma Makutsi had not expected this, and the sight of this woman behind the desk deprived her of all the poise she had summoned for her entry. But in that respect she was equal with the woman behind the desk; equal in other respects, too, as it was her old class-mate from the Botswana Secretarial College, Violet Sephotho.

It was Violet who recovered first. 'Well, well,' she said. 'Grace Makutsi. First the College. Then the Academy of Dance and Movement. Now here. All these crossings of our paths, Mma! Perhaps we shall even find out now that we are cousins!'

'That would be a surprise, Mma,' said Mma Makutsi, without saying what sort of surprise it would be.

'I was only joking,' said Violet. 'I do not think we are cousins. But that is not the point. The point is that you have come here looking for a job? Is that correct?'

Mma Makutsi opened her mouth to reply, but Violet continued. 'You must have heard of us. We are what are called head hunters these days. We find top people for top jobs.'

'It must be interesting work,' said Mma Makutsi. 'I wondered whether . . .'

'It is,' said Violet. 'Very interesting.' She paused, looking quizzically at Mma Makutsi. 'I thought, though, that you had a good job,' she went on. 'Don't you work for that fat woman who runs that detective business next to that smelly old garage? Don't you work for her?'

'That is Mma Ramotswe,' said Mma Makutsi. 'And the garage is Tlokweng Road Speedy Motors. It is run by . . .'

Violet interrupted. 'Yes, yes,' she said impatiently. 'So you've lost that job, have you?'

Mma Makutsi gasped. It was outrageous that this Violet, this fifty-per-cent (at the most) person should imagine that she had been dismissed from the No. 1 Ladies' Detective Agency. 'I did not!' she burst out. 'I did not lose that job, Mma! I left of my own accord.'

Violet looked at her unapologetically. 'Of course, Mma. Of course. Although sometimes people leave just before they're pushed. Not you, of course, but that happens, you know.'

Mma Makutsi took a deep breath. If she allowed herself to become angered, or at least to show her anger, then she would be playing directly into Violet's hands. So she smiled gently and nodded her agreement with Violet's comment. 'Yes, Mma. There are many cases of people who are dismissed who say that they resigned. You must see a lot of that. But I really did resign because I wanted a change. That's why I'm here.'

This submissive tone seemed to appeal to Violet. She looked at Mma Makutsi thoughtfully. 'I'll see what I can do,' she said slowly. 'But I can't work miracles. The problem is that ... Well, the problem, Mma, is one of *presentation*. These days it is very important that firms have a smart image. It's all about impact, you know. And that means that senior staff must be well presented, must be ... of good appearance. That's the way it is in business these days. That's just the way it is.' She shuffled a few papers on her desk. 'There are a few high-level vacancies at the moment. A personal assistant post to a chief executive. A secretary to the general manager of a bank. That sort of thing.

108

But I'm not sure if you're quite right for that sort of job, Mma. Maybe something in a Ministry somewhere. Or . . .' She paused. 'Have you thought of leaving Gaborone? Of taking something down in Lobatse or Francistown or somewhere like that? Lots of people like those places, you know. There's not so much going on, of course, but it's a peaceful life out of town.'

Mma Makutsi watched Violet as she spoke. The face revealed so much; that she had been taught by Mma Ramotswe, who had pointed out that the real meaning of what anybody said was written large in the muscles of the face. And Violet's face said it all; this was a calculated put-down, an intentional humiliation, possibly inspired by jealousy (Violet knew about Phuti Radiphuti and knew that he was well off), possibly inspired by anger over their vastly differing performances at the Botswana Secretarial College, but more probably inspired by pure malice, which was something which often just occurred in people for no apparent reason and with which there was no reasoning.

She rose to her feet. 'I don't think you have anything suitable for me,' she said.

Violet became flustered. 'I didn't say that, Mma.'

'I think you did, Mma,' said Mma Makutsi. 'I think you said it very clearly. Sometimes people don't have to open their mouths to say anything, but they say it nonetheless.'

She moved towards the door. For a moment or two it seemed as if Violet was about to say something, but she did not. Mma Makutsi gave her one last glance, and then left, nodding to the receptionist on her way out, as politeness dictated. Mma Ramotswe would be proud of me, she thought; Mma Ramotswe had always said that the repaying of rudeness with rudeness was the wrong thing to do as it taught the other person no lesson. And she was right about that, as she was right about so many other things. Mma Ramotswe . . . Mma Makutsi saw the face of her friend and heard her voice, as if she was right there, beside her. She would have laughed at Violet. She would have said of her insults, *Little words, Mma, from an unhappy woman. Nothing to think twice about. Nothing.*

Mma Makutsi went out into the sunshine, composed herself, and began to walk home. The sun was high now, and there was much more warmth in it. She could get a minibus most of the way, if she waited, but she decided to walk, and had gone only a short distance when the heel of her right shoe broke. The shoe now flapped uselessly, and she had to take both shoes off. At home, in Bobonong, she had often gone barefoot, and it was no great hardship now. But it had not been a good morning, that morning, and she felt miserable.

She walked on. Near the stretch of open bush that the school used for playing sports, she picked up a thorn in her right foot. It was easy to extract, but it pricked hard for such a small thing. She sat down on a stone and nursed her foot, rubbing it to relieve the pain. She looked up at the sky. If there were people up there, she did not think that they cared for people down here. There were no thorns up there, no rudeness, no broken shoes.

She rose and picked up her shoes. As she did so, a rattly old blue taxi drove past, the driver with his right arm resting casually on the sill of the window. She thought for a moment, *That's a dangerous thing*

110

to do—another car might drive too close and that would be the end of your arm.

She raised her own arm, suddenly, on impulse. The taxi stopped.

'Tlokweng Road, please,' she said. 'You know that old garage? That place. The No. 1 Ladies' Detective Agency.'

'I will take you there, Mma,' said the taxi driver. He was not rude. He was polite, and he made conversation with Mma Makutsi as they drove.

'Why are you going there, Mma?' he asked as they negotiated the lights at the old four-way stop.

'Because that's where I work,' said Mma Makutsi. 'I took the morning off. Now it's time to go back.'

She looked down at the broken shoe, now resting on her lap. It was such a sad thing, that shoe, like a body from which the life had gone. She stared at it. Almost challenging it to reproach her. But it did not, and all she heard, she thought, was a strangled voice which said, *Narrow escape, Boss. You were walking in the wrong direction, you know. We shoes understand these things.*

*   *   *

If it had been a bleak morning for Mma Makutsi, it was equally bleak at the premises of the No. 1 Ladies' Detective Agency and Tlokweng Road Speedy Motors. In Mma Ramotswe's small office the desk previously occupied by Mma Makutsi stood forlorn, bare of paper, with only a couple of pencils and an abandoned typewriter upon it. Where three cups had stood on the cabinet behind it, along with the tea-making equipment of a kettle and two tea-pots, there now were only two—Mma Ramotswe's personal cup and the cup that was kept for the client. The absence of Mma Makutsi's cup, a small thing in itself but a big thing in what it stood for, seemed only to confirm in Mma Ramotswe's view that the heart had been taken out of the office. Steps could be taken, of course: Mr Polopetsi could be invited to keep his mug there rather than on the hook which it occupied beside the spanners in the garage. But it would not be the same; indeed it was impossible to imagine Mr Polopetsi occupying Mma Makutsi's chair; much as Mma Ramotswe liked him, he was a man, and the whole ethos of the No. 1 Ladies' Detective Agency, its guiding principle really, was that it was a business in which women were in the driving seat. That was not because men could not do the job— they could, provided they were the right sort of men, observant men—it was simply because that particular business had always been run by women, and it was women who gave it its particular style. There was room in this world, Mma Ramotswe thought, for things done by men and things done by women; sometimes men could do the things done by women, sometimes not. And vice versa, of course.

She felt lonely. In spite of the sounds from the garage, in spite of the fact that immediately on the other side of the office wall was Mr J.L.B. Matekoni, her husband and help-mate, she felt alone, bereft. She had once been told by an aunt in Mochudi how, shortly after being widowed, she had seen her husband in empty rooms, in places where he liked to sit in the sun, coming back down the track that he always walked down; and these were not tricks of the light, but aches of the mind, its sad longings. And now, after her assistant had been absent for so short a time, she had looked up suddenly when she thought she heard Mma Makutsi say something, or had seen something move on the other side of the room. That movement was a real trick of the light of course, but it still brought home the fact that she was on her own now.

And that was difficult. Mma Ramotswe was normally quite content with her own company. She could sit on her verandah on Zebra Drive and drink tea in perfect solitude, with her only company that of the birds outside, or of the tiny, scrambling geckos that made their way up the pillars and across the roof; that was different. In an office one needed to be able to talk to somebody, if only to make the surroundings more human. Homes, verandahs, gardens were human in their feel; offices were not. An office with only one person in it was a place unfurnished.

On the other side of the wall, Mr J.L.B. Matekoni felt a similar moroseness. It was perhaps not quite as acute in his case, but it was still there, a feeling that somehow things were not complete. It was as a family might feel, he thought, if it sat down to dinner on some great occasion and had one seat unoccupied. He liked Mma Makutsi; he had always admired her determination and her courage. He would not like to cross her, of course, as she could be prickly, and he was not sure whether she handled the apprentices very well. In fact she did not; he was certain of it, but he had never quite got round to suggesting to her that she should change her tone when handling those admittedly frustrating young men. And of course Charlie was going to go too, once he had finished tinkering with that old Mercedes and the taxi licence application had been approved. The garage would not be the same without him, Mr J.L.B. Matekoni thought; there would be something missing, in spite of everything.

Charlie, from the other side of the garage, where he was about to raise a car on the hydraulic ramp, glanced at Mr J.L.B. Matekoni and said to the younger apprentice, standing beside him, 'I hope that the Boss doesn't think that she's gone because of me. I hope he doesn't think that.'

The younger apprentice wiped his nose on the sleeve of his blue overalls. 'Why would he think that, Charlie? What's it got to do with you? You know what that woman's like. Nag, nag, nag. I bet that the Boss is relieved that she's gone.'

Charlie thought about this possibility for a moment, and then dismissed it. 'He likes her. Mma Ramotswe likes her too. Maybe even you like her.' He looked at the younger man and frowned. 'Do you? Do you like her?'

The younger apprentice shifted his feet. 'I don't like her glasses,' he said. 'Where do you think she got those great big glasses?'

'An industrial catalogue,' said Charlie.

The younger apprentice laughed. 'And those stupid shoes of hers. She thinks she looks good in those shoes of hers, but most girls I know wouldn't be seen dead in them.'

Charlie looked thoughtful. 'They take your shoes off when you're dead, you know.'

The younger apprentice was concerned. 'Why?' he asked. 'What do they do with them?'

Charlie reached forward and polished the dial of the panel that controlled the hydraulic lift. 'The doctors take them,' he explained. 'Or the nurses in the hospital. Next time you see a doctor, look at his shoes. They all have very smart shoes. Lots of them. That's because they get the shoes when . . .'

He stopped. A blue taxi had drawn up in front of the garage and the passenger door was opening.

CHAPTER TEN

A Small Businesswoman

With Mma Makutsi back in her usual place, the heavy atmosphere that had prevailed that morning lifted. The emotional reunion, as demonstrative and effusive as if Mma Makutsi had been away for months, or even years, had embarrassed the men, who had exchanged glances, and then looked away, as if in guilt at an intrusion into essentially female mysteries. But when the ululating from Mma Ramotswe had died down and the tea had been made, everything returned to normal.

'Why did she bother to leave if she was going to be away five minutes?' asked the younger apprentice.

'It's because she doesn't think like anybody else,' said Charlie. 'She thinks backwards.'

Mr J.L.B. Matekoni, who overheard this, shook his head. 'It's a sign of maturity to be able to change your mind when you realise that you're wrong,' he explained. 'It's the same with fixing a car. If you find out that you're going along the wrong lines, then don't hesitate to stop and correct yourself. If, for example, you're changing the oil seal at the back of a gearbox, you might try to save time by doing this without taking the gearbox out. But it's always quicker to take the gearbox out. If you don't, you end up taking the floor out and anyway you have to take the top of the gearbox off, and the prop shaft too. So it's best to stop and admit your mistake before you go any further and damage things.'

Charlie listened to this—it was a long speech for Mr J.L.B. Matekoni—and then looked away. He wondered if this was a random example seized upon by Mr J.L.B. Matekoni, or if he knew about that seal he had tried to install in the old rear-wheel-drive Ford. Could he have found out somehow?

There was little work done in the agency that afternoon. Mma Makutsi restored her desk to the way she liked it to be: papers reappeared, pencils were resharpened and arranged in the right fashion, and files were extracted from the cabinet and placed back on the desk for further attention. Mma Ramotswe watched all this with utter satisfaction and, after she had offered to make the tea—an offer which Mma Makutsi politely declined, pointing out that she had not forgotten her role altogether—she asked her assistant if she would care to have the rest of the afternoon off.

'You may have shopping to do, Mma,' said Mma Ramotswe. 'You know that you can have the time off whenever you want for things like that.'

Mma Makutsi had clearly been pleased by this, but again declined. There was filing to do, she insisted; it was extraordinary how quickly filing accumulated; one turned one's back for a few hours and there it was—piled up. Mma Ramotswe thought that this was also true of detection work. 'No sooner do you deal with one case,' she said, 'than another turns up. There is somebody coming tomorrow morning. I should really be seeing people about that hospital matter, but I am going to have to be here to see this other person. Unless . . .'

She glanced across the room at Mma Makutsi, who was polishing her spectacles with that threadbare lace handkerchief of hers. You would think, Mma Ramotswe said to herself, that she would buy herself a new handkerchief now that she had the money, but people held on to things they loved; they just did.

Mma Makutsi finished with her polishing and replaced her large round spectacles. She looked straight at Mma Ramotswe. 'Unless?'

Mma Ramotswe had always insisted that she see the client first, even if the matter was subsequently to be delegated to Mma Makutsi. But things had to change, and perhaps this was the time to do it. Mma Makutsi could be made an associate detective and given the chance to deal with clients herself, right from the beginning of a case. All that would be required would be that the client's chair be turned round to face Mma Makutsi's desk rather than hers.

'Unless you, as . . . as associate detective were to interview the client yourself and look after the whole matter.' Mma Ramotswe paused. The afternoon sun was slanting in through the window and had fallen on Mma Makutsi's head, glinting off her spectacles.

'Of course,' said Mma Makutsi quietly. Associate detective. Whole matter. Herself. 'Of course,' she repeated. 'That would be possible. Tomorrow morning? Of course, Mma. You leave it to me.'

*   *   *

The small woman sitting in the re-oriented client's chair looked at Mma Makutsi. 'Mma?'

'Makutsi. I am Grace Makutsi.'

'I had heard that there was a woman called Mma Ramotswe. People have spoken of her. I heard very good things.'

'There is a woman of that name,' said Mma Makutsi. 'She is my colleague.' She faltered briefly at the word *colleague*. Of course Mma Ramotswe was her colleague; she was also her employer, but there was nothing to say that an employer could not also be a colleague. She went on, 'We work very closely together. As associates. So that is why you are seeing me. She is out on another case.'

The small woman hesitated for a moment, but then appeared to accept that situation. She leaned forward in her chair, and Mma Makutsi noticed how her expression seemed to be a pleading one, the expression of one who wanted something very badly. 'My name, Mma, is Mma Magama, but nobody calls me that very much. They call me Teenie.'

'That is because ...' Mma Makutsi stopped herself.

'That is because I have always been called that,' said Teenie. 'Teenie is a good name for a small person, you see, Mma.'

118

'You are not so small, Mma,' said Mma Makutsi. But you are, she thought; you're terribly small.

'I have seen some smaller people,' said Teenie appreciatively.

'Where did you see them?' asked Mma Makutsi. She had not intended to ask the question, but it slipped out.

Teenie pointed vaguely out of the window, but said nothing.

'Anyway, Mma,' Mma Makutsi went on. 'Perhaps you will tell me why you have come to see us.'

Mma Makutsi watched Teenie's eyes as she spoke. The pleading look that accompanied each sentence was disconcerting.

'I have a business, you see, Mma,' Teenie said. 'It is a good business. It is a printing works. There are ten people who work there. Ten. People look at me and think that I am too small to have a business like that—they look surprised. But what difference does it make, Mma? What difference?'

Mma Makutsi shrugged. 'No difference at all, Mma. Some people are very stupid.'

Teenie agreed with this. 'Very,' she said. 'What matters is what's up here.' She tapped her head. Mma Makutsi could not help but notice that her head was very small too. Did the size of a brain have any bearing on its ability? she wondered. Chickens had very small brains but elephants had much bigger ones, and there was a difference.

'I started the business with my late husband,' Teenie went on. 'He was run over on the Lobatse Road eleven years ago.'

Mma Makutsi lowered her eyes. He must have been small too; perhaps the driver just did not see him. 'I am sorry, Mma. That was very sad.'

'Yes,' said Teenie. 'But I had to get on with my life and so I carried on with the business. I built it up. I bought a new German printing machine which made us one of the cheapest places in the country to print anything. Full colour. Laminates. Everything, Mma.'

'That is very good,' said Mma Makutsi.

'We could do you a calendar for yourselves next year,' said Teenie, looking at the almost bare walls, but noticing, appreciatively, the display of her own calendar. 'I see that somebody has given you our calendar up there. You will see how well printed it is. Or we could do some business cards. Have you got a business card, Mma?'

The answer was no, but the idea was implanted. If one was an associate detective, then perhaps one was expected to have a business card. Mma Ramotswe herself did not have one, but that was more to do with her traditional views than with cost.

'I would like to have one,' said Mma Makutsi. 'And I would like you to print it for me.'

'We shall do that,' said Teenie. 'We can take the cost off your fee.'

That was not what Mma Makutsi had intended, but now she was committed. She indicated to Teenie that she should continue with her story.

Teenie moved forward in her seat. Mma Makutsi saw that her client's feet barely touched the floor in front of her. 'I look after the people who work for me very well,' said Teenie. 'I never ask people to work longer hours than they want to. Everybody gets three weeks' holiday on full pay. After two years, everybody gets a bonus. Two years only, Mma! In some places you wait ten years for a bonus.'

'Your people must be very happy,' said Mma Makutsi. 'It's not everybody who is as good to their staff as you are.'

'That is true,' said Teenie. She frowned before continuing. 'But then if they are so happy, why do I have somebody who is stealing from me? That is what I cannot understand—I really can't. They are stealing supplies. Paper. Inks. The supply cupboards are always half-empty.'

From the moment that Teenie mentioned staff, Mma Makutsi had anticipated this. It was one of the commonest complaints that clients brought to the No. 1 Ladies' Detective Agency, although not quite as common as the errant husband complaint. Botswana was not a dishonest country—quite the contrary, really—but it was inevitable that there would be some who would cheat and steal and do all the unhelpful and unpleasant things that humanity was heir to. That had started a long time back, at the point at which some Eden somewhere had gone wrong, and somebody had picked up a stone and hurled it at another. It was in us, thought Mma Makutsi; it was in all of us, somewhere deep down in our very nature. When we were children we had to be taught to hold it in check, to banish it; we had to be taught to be concerned with the feelings of others. And that, she thought, was where things went wrong. Some children were just not taught, or would not learn, or were governed by some impulse within them that stopped them from feeling and understanding. Later on, there was very little one could do about these people, other than to thwart them. Mma Ramotswe, of course, said that you could be kind to them, to

121

show them the way, but Mma Makutsi had her doubts about that; one could be too kind, she thought.

'People steal,' said Mma Makutsi. 'No matter how kind you are to them, there are some people who will steal. Even from their own family, in their own house. That happens, you know.'

Teenie fixed her pleading eyes on Mma Makutsi. It occurred to Mma Makutsi that the woman in front of her wanted her to say that people did not steal, that the world was not a place where this sort of thing happened. She could not give her that reassurance, because, well, because it would be absurd. One could not say the world was other than it was.

'I'm sorry about that,' Mma Makutsi went on. 'It obviously makes you unhappy, Mma.'

Teenie was quick to agree. 'It's like being hurt somewhere here,' she said, moving her hand to her chest and placing it above the sternum. 'It's a horrible feeling. This thief is not a person who comes at night and takes from you—it's somebody you see every day, who smiles at you, who asks how you have slept; all of that. It is one of your brothers or sisters.'

Mma Makutsi could see that. She had been stolen from when she was at the Botswana Secretarial College. Somebody in the class had taken her purse, which contained all her money for that week, which was not very much anyway, but which was needed, every thebe of it. Once that was gone, there was no money for food, and she would have to depend on the help of others. Did the person who took the purse *know* that? Would that person *care* if he or she knew that the loss of the money would mean hunger?

'It always hurts,' she said. There had been two days of hunger because she had been too proud to ask, and then a friend, who had heard what had happened, had shared her food with her.

Mma Makutsi folded her hands; they would have to progress from these observations on the human condition to the business in hand. 'You would like me to find out who is doing this?' She paused and stared at Teenie with a serious look; it would be best for her to know that these things were far from easy. 'When something is being stolen by somebody on the inside,' she said, 'it is not always easy. In fact, it can be very hard to discover who is doing it. We have to look at who's spending what, at who's living beyond their means. That's one way. But it can be hard . . .'

Teenie interrupted her. The pleading look now became something more confident. 'No, Mma,' she said. 'It will not be hard. It will not be hard because I can tell you who is doing it. I know exactly who it is.'

Mma Makutsi could not conceal her surprise. 'Oh yes?'

'Yes. I can point to the person who's stealing. I know exactly who it is.'

Well, thought Mma Makutsi, if she knows who is responsible, then what is there for me to do? 'So, Mma,' she said. 'What do you want me to do? It seems that you have already been a detective.'

Teenie took this in her stride. 'I cannot prove anything,' she said. 'I know who it is, but I have no proof. That is what I want you to find for me. Proof. Then I can get rid of that person. The employment laws say: proof first, then dismissal.'

Mma Makutsi smiled. Clovis Andersen in *The Principles of Private Detection* had something to say about this, she recalled—as had Mma Ramotswe. *You do not know anything until you know why you know it*, he had written. And Mma Ramotswe, who had read the passage out to Mma Makutsi with an admonitory wagging of her finger, had qualified this by saying that although this was generally true, sometimes she knew that she knew something because of a special feeling that she had. But what Clovis Andersen said was nonetheless correct, she felt.

'You will have to tell me why you think you know who it is,' Mma Makutsi said to Teenie. 'Have you seen this person taking something?'

Teenie thought for a moment. 'Not exactly.'

'Ah.'

There was a short period of silence. 'Has anybody else seen this person taking something?' Mma Makutsi went on.

Teenie shook her head. 'No. Not as far as I know.'

'So, may I ask you, Mma: how do you know who this person is?'

Teenie closed her eyes. 'Because of the way he looks, Mma. This man who is taking things, he just looks dishonest. He is not a nice man. I can tell that, Mma.'

Mma Makutsi reached for a piece of paper and wrote down a few words. Teenie watched the pencil move across the paper, then she looked up expectantly at Mma Makutsi.

'I shall need to come and have a look round,' said Mma Makutsi. 'You must not tell the staff that I am a detective. We shall have to think of some

124

reason for me to be visiting the works.'

'You could be a tax inspector,' ventured Teenie.

Mma Makutsi laughed. 'That is a very bad idea,' she said. 'They will think that I am after them. No, you can say that I am a client who is interested in giving the firm a big job but who wants to have a good look at how things are run. That will be a good story.'

Teenie agreed with this. And would Mma Makutsi be available that afternoon? Everybody, including the man under suspicion, would be there and she could meet them all.

'How will I know which is the one you suspect?' asked Mma Makutsi.

'You'll know,' said Teenie. 'The moment you see him. You'll know.'

She looked at Mma Makutsi. Still pleading.

CHAPTER ELEVEN

Dr Cronje

While Mma Makutsi dealt with her diminutive client, Mma Ramotswe made the brief drive out to Mochudi; forty minutes if one rushed, an hour if one meandered. And she did meander, slowing down to look at some cattle who had strayed onto the verge of the road. She was her father's daughter after all, and Obed Ramotswe had never been able to pass by cattle without casting his expert eye over them. She had inherited some of that ability, a gift really, even if her eye would never be as good as his had been. He had cattle

125

lineages embedded in his memory, like a biblical narrative setting out who begat whom; he knew every beast and their qualities. And she had always dreamed that when he died, at the very moment at which that bit of the old Botswana went, the cattle had somehow known. She understood that this was impossible, that it was sentimental, but the thought had given her comfort. When we die there are many farewells, spoken and unspoken—and the imagined farewell of the cattle was one of these.

The cattle by the roadside were not in particularly good condition, Mma Ramotswe thought. There was little grazing for them at this time of the year, with the rains a few months away and such grass as there was dry and brittle. The cattle would find something, of course, leaves, bits and pieces of vegetation that would provide some sustenance; but these beasts looked defeated and listless. They would not have a good owner, Mma Ramotswe concluded as she continued on her journey. To start with, they should not be out on the verge like that. Not only was that a risk to the cattle themselves, but it was a terrible danger to anybody driving on the road at night. Some cattle were the colour of night and seemed to merge perfectly into the darkness; a driver coming round a corner or surmounting a hump in the road might suddenly find himself face-to-face with one of these cattle and be unable to stop in time. If that happened, then those in the car could be impaled on the horns of the cow as it was hurled through the windscreen—that had happened, and often. Mma Ramotswe shuddered, and concentrated on the winding strip of tar ahead. Cattle, goats, children, other drivers—there were so many perils on the road.

By the time she arrived in Mochudi, her dawdling on the road had made her late. She looked at her watch. It was twelve o'clock and she had arranged to meet the doctor at a restaurant on the edge of the town fifteen minutes earlier; he had to have an early lunch, he explained, as he would be on duty at the hospital at two. She wondered if he would wait; she had telephoned him out of the blue and asked to see him—there were many who would decline an invitation of that sort, but he had agreed without any probing into what her business with him might be. All she had said was that she was a friend of Tati Monyena; that, it seemed, was enough.

Mochudi had a number of restaurants, most of them very small affairs, one small room at the most, or a rickety bench outside a lean-to shack serving braised maize cobs and plates of pap; simple fare, but filling and delicious. Then there were the liquor restaurants, which were larger and noisier. Some of these stayed one step ahead of the police and the tribal authorities, and were regularly being closed down for the disturbance they created and their cavalier attitude to licensing hours. Mma Ramotswe did not like these, with their dark interiors and their groups of drinkers engaged in endless and heated debates over their bottles of beer; that was not for her.

There was one good restaurant, though, one that she liked, which had a garden and tables in that garden. The kitchens were clean, the food wholesome, and the waitresses adept at friendly conversation. She went there from time to time when she felt that she needed to catch up on

Mochudi news, and she would spin out her lunch to two or three hours, talking or just sitting under one of the trees and looking up at the birds on the branches above. It was a good place for birds, a bird restaurant, and the more confident amongst their number would flutter down to the ground to peck at the crumbs of food under the tables, minute zebra finches, bulbuls, plain birds that had no name as far as she knew.

The tiny white van drew up in front of the restaurant and Mma Ramotswe alighted. A wide acacia tree stood at the entrance to the restaurant garden, an umbrella against the sun, and a dog sat just outside the lacy shadow of the tree, his eyes half closed, soaking up the winter sun. A couple of flies walked across the narrow part of his nose, but he did not flinch. Mma Ramotswe saw that only one of the outside tables was occupied, and she knew immediately that it was the doctor. Half Xhosa, half Afrikaner. It could only be him.

'Dr Cronje?'

The doctor looked up from the photocopied article he had been reading. Mma Ramotswe noticed the graphs across the page, the tables of results. Behind the things that happened to one, the coughs and pains, the human fevers, there were these cold figures.

He started to rise to his feet, but Mma Ramotswe urged him not to. 'I am sorry to be late. It is my fault. I drove very slowly.' She noticed that the doctor had green eyes; green eyes and a skin that was very light brown, the colour of chocolate milk, a mixture of Africa and Europe.

'Drive slowly,' he mused. 'If only everyone would do that, we'd be less busy in the hospital, Mma

Ramotswe.'

A waitress appeared and took their order. He put his papers away in a small folder and then turned his gaze to Mma Ramotswe. 'Mr Monyena told us that you might want to speak to people,' he said. 'So here I am. He's the boss.'

He spoke politely enough, but there was a flatness in his tone. That explains it, thought Mma Ramotswe. That explains why he came.

'So he told you that I have been asked to look into those unexplained deaths,' she said. 'Did he tell you that?'

'Yes,' he said. 'Though why we need anybody else to do that beats me. We had an internal enquiry, you know. Mr Monyena was on that himself. Why have another one?'

Mma Ramotswe was interested. Tati Monyena had not told her about an internal enquiry, which must have been an oversight on his part.

'And what did it conclude?' she asked.

Dr Cronje rolled his eyes up in a gesture which indicated contempt for internal enquiries. 'Nothing,' he said. 'Absolutely nothing. The trouble was that some people could not bring themselves to admit the obvious. So the enquiry petered out. Technically it hasn't been wound up.'

The waitress now brought them their drinks: a pot of bush tea for Mma Ramotswe and a cup of coffee for the doctor. Mma Ramotswe poured her tea and took a first sip.

'What do you think it should have decided?' she asked. 'What if you had been on it?'

The doctor smiled—for the first time, thought Mma Ramotswe—and it was not a smile that lasted long.

'I was,' he said.

'You were?'

'I was a member of the enquiry. It was the hospital superintendant, Mr Monyena, one of the senior staff nurses, somebody nominated by Chief Linchwe, and me. That was it.'

Mma Ramotswe took another sip of tea. Somebody had started to play music inside the restaurant, and for a few seconds she thought she recognised the tune as one that had been played by Note Mokoti, her former husband. She caught her breath; Note was over, gone, but when she heard his music, the tunes he liked to play, which she sometimes did, a tinge of pain could come. But it was a different tune, something like one that he played, but different.

'When you say that there was something very obvious that people could not admit, what was that, Rra?'

The doctor reached out and touched the rim of his coffee cup, idly drawing a finger round it. 'Natural causes,' he said. 'Cardiac and pulmonary failure in two of the cases. Renal in the other. Case closed, Mma . . . Mma . . .'

He had already used her name, but she supplied it again. 'Ramotswe.'

'Ramotswe. Sorry.'

They sat in silence for a moment. Then the doctor looked up into the tree, as if trying to find something. She saw the green eyes moving, searching. The green eyes were from the Afrikaner, but the softness of his face, a masculine softness but a softness nonetheless, came from the mother, came from Africa.

'So there's really nothing further to be done

130

about it,' Mma Ramotswe said gently.

The doctor did not reply for a moment; he was still looking up into the tree above them. 'In my view, no,' he said. 'But that won't stop the talk, the pointing of fingers.'

'At?' asked Mma Ramotswe.

'Me,' he said. He looked down again and their eyes met. 'Yes, me. There are people in the hospital who say that I'm bad luck. They look at me in that way ... you know, that way which people use here. As if they're a bit frightened of you. They say nothing, but they look.'

It was hard for Mma Ramotswe to respond to this. She had a sense that Dr Cronje was one of those people who did not fit in—wherever they were. They were outsiders, treated with a reserve which could easily become suspicion, and that suspicion could easily blossom into a whispering campaign of ugly rumours. But what puzzled her was why she herself should have this uneasy feeling about him, which she did. Why should she feel this discomfort in his presence when she knew next to nothing about him? It was intuition again; useful sometimes but on other occasions a doubtful benefit.

'People are like that,' she said at last. 'If you come from somewhere else, they can be like that. It is not easy to be a stranger, is it?'

He looked at her as she spoke; it seemed to her that he was surprised that she should speak like this, with such frankness. 'No,' he said, and then paused before he continued. 'And that is what I have been all my life. All of it.'

The waitress arrived with their plates. There was stew, and a plate of vegetables for each of them.

He looked at his plate. 'I shouldn't talk like this, Mma. I have nothing to complain about, really. This is a good place.'

Mma Ramotswe lifted up her fork, and then put it down again. She reached across and laid a hand upon his wrist. He looked down at where her hand rested.

'You mustn't be sad, Rra,' she said.

He frowned, and laid down his knife.

'I wish I could go home,' he said. 'I love this country. I love it. But it's not home for me.'

'Well you could go home,' Mma Ramotswe said. She nodded in the direction of the border, not far across a few miles of scrub bush, behind the hills. 'You could go home now, couldn't you? There's nothing stopping you.'

'That place is not home any more,' he said. 'I left it so long ago, I don't feel at home there.'

'And this place? Here?'

'It's where I live. But I can't ever belong here, can I? I will never be from this place. I will never be one of these people, no matter how long I stay. I'll always be an outsider.'

She knew what he meant. It was all very well for her, she thought; she knew exactly where she came from and where she belonged, but there were many people who did not, who had been uprooted, forced out by need or victimisation, by being simply the wrong people in the wrong place. There were many such people in Africa, and they ate a very bitter fruit; they were extra, unwanted persons, like children who are not loved.

She wanted to say something to this man, this lonely doctor, but she realised there was little comfort she could give him. Yet she could try.

132

'Don't think, Rra,' she said, 'that what you are doing, your work in the hospital up there, is not appreciated. Nobody might ever have said thank you to you, but I do now, Rra. I say thank you for what you do.'

He had lowered his gaze, but now he looked at her, and she found herself staring into those unnerving green eyes.

'Thank you, Mma,' he said. And then he picked up his knife and fork and began to eat.

Mma Ramotswe watched discreetly as she started on her own plate of food. She saw the way his knife moved, delicately, with precision.

*   *   *

Mr J.L.B. Matekoni talked to Charlie that afternoon.

'You can stop work today, Charlie,' he said. 'I have made up your final pay packet.'

Charlie wiped his hands on a piece of paper towel. 'This stuff isn't as good as lint, Boss,' he said, frowning at the towel. 'Lint gets grease off much better.'

'Paper towel is the modern thing,' said Mr J.L.B. Matekoni. 'Paper towel and that scouring powder. That is very good for grease.'

'Well, I won't need that any more,' said Charlie. 'Except maybe when I service the taxi.'

'Don't forget to do that,' warned Mr J.L.B. Matekoni. 'It is an old car. Those old cars need regular oil changes. So change your oil every two months, Charlie. You will never regret that.'

The apprentice beamed with pleasure. 'I will, Boss.'

133

Mr J.L.B. Matekoni looked at him from under his eyebrows. He doubted that the car would be well looked after, but he had steeled himself to let Charlie get on with his plans. And now it had come to the point where he would say goodbye and hand over the car. There was an agreement to be signed, of course, because Charlie did not have the money to pay for the vehicle and it would have to be paid off month by month for almost three years. Even then, he wondered whether he would ever see the money, or all of it, as of the two apprentices Charlie had always been the more financially irresponsible one and always tried to borrow towards the end of the month when money got tight.

Charlie glanced at the document which Mr J.L.B. Matekoni had drawn up and that had been typed out by Mma Makutsi that afternoon. He would pay six hundred pula a month until the cost of the car had been covered. He would make sure that it was insured. If he could not keep up the payments he would give the car back to Mr J.L.B. Matekoni, who would pay the book price for it. That was all.

'You should read that carefully,' said Mr J.L.B. Matekoni. 'It is a legal document, you know.'

But Charlie reached out for a pen from his employer's top pocket. He left a small grease stain on the edge of the fabric. 'That's fine by me, Boss,' he said. 'You would never try to cheat me. I know that. You are my father.'

Mr J.L.B. Matekoni watched Charlie as he signed with a flourish and handed over the piece of paper. There were greasy fingerprints on the document where the apprentice had held it. I have tried to teach him, Mr J.L.B. Matekoni said to himself. I have tried my best.

They went outside to where the old Mercedes-Benz was parked. Mr J.L.B. Matekoni handed over the keys to Charlie. 'It's insured on my policy for the next two weeks,' he said. 'Then it's up to you.'

Charlie looked at the keys. 'I can hardly believe this, Boss. I can hardly believe it.'

Mr J.L.B. Matekoni bit his lip. He had looked after this boy, every day, every day, for years now. 'I know you'll do your best, Charlie,' he said quietly. 'I know that.'

A door opened in the building behind them and Mma Makutsi appeared. Charlie put the keys in his pocket and looked nervously at Mr J.L.B. Matekoni.

'I have come to say goodbye,' Mma Makutsi said. 'And to wish you good luck with the business, Charlie. I hope that it goes well with you.'

Charlie had been staring at the ground. Now he looked up and smiled. 'Thank you, Mma. I will try.'

'Yes,' said Mma Makutsi. 'I am sure that you will. And here's another thing. I'm sorry, Rra, if I have ever been unkind to you. I am sorry for that.'

Nobody spoke. Mr J.L.B. Matekoni, who was holding the piece of paper which Charlie had signed, busied himself with folding it neatly and putting it into his pocket, a task which seemed to take a long time, and had to be re-done. Somewhere, on the road behind the garage, an engine revved up, coughed, and then died away into silence.

'That needs fixing,' said Charlie, laughing nervously. Then, he looked at Mma Makutsi, and smiled at her. 'If you need my taxi, Mma,' he said,

'I will be proud to drive you.'

'And I will be proud to go in it,' she said. 'Thank you.'

After that, there was little more to be said. Great feuds often need very few words to resolve them. Disputes, even between nations, between peoples, can be set to rest with simple acts of contrition and corresponding forgiveness, can so often be shown to be based on nothing much other than pride and misunderstanding, and the forgetting of the humanity of the other—and land, of course.

CHAPTER TWELVE

A Gift from Mr Phuti Radiphuti

After the departure of Charlie, which happened shortly after four o'clock, Mr J.L.B. Matekoni found it difficult to settle back to work. Charlie had driven away in triumph, at the wheel of the Mercedes-Benz which Mr J.L.B. Matekoni had just made over to him. For the proprietor of Tlokweng Road Speedy Motors it was an emotional parting, and although Mr J.L.B. Matekoni was not one to show his feelings—mechanics do not do that—he had nearly been overcome by the moment. When he had first taken on the two apprentices, he had allowed himself to imagine that perhaps one of them would prove to be his helpmate and would in due course take over the garage. Charlie would have been the obvious choice, as the older of the two boys, but before very long it had become apparent to Mr J.L.B. Matekoni that such thoughts were no more than fond imaginings. But in spite of all Charlie's faults—his bad workmanship, his impetuosity, his endless attempts to impress girls—Mr J.L.B. Matekoni had conceived of a rough affection for him, as one will sometimes grow to love another for his human weaknesses. Now, with Charlie away, and the younger apprentice looking lost and disconsolate, Mr J.L.B. Matekoni felt curiously empty. It was not that he had no work to do—a station wagon belonging to an Air Botswana pilot, a much-loved car which Mr J.L.B. Matekoni had nursed through various mechanical illnesses, was waiting for him to replace some of its wiring. The old wires, pulled out and unravelled like a network of nerves, protruded from their hiding places; fuses lay beside them on the seats. But he could not bring himself to start this task, and so he put it off until the next day.

Now he would return to his other role—to the investigation of the errant Mr Botumile. His last observation of this man had revealed nothing more than that he kept surprisingly bad company. But that was not the same thing as adultery, and it was a suspected affair that had brought Mma Botumile to the door of the No. 1 Ladies' Detective Agency. She wanted to know the identity of the woman whom she suspected her husband was seeing—a reasonable thing for a wife to want to know, thought Mr J.L.B. Matekoni—and he was determined to find that out. What happened after that was another matter. Mma Botumile was a formidable person, and Mr J.L.B. Matekoni did not envy the other woman any encounter that she might have with her. That was not really his business, though. At the most, he imagined that he or Mma Ramotswe might be asked to warn the girlfriend off, which was something that could be done quite tactfully. All that would be necessary, he thought, would be to tell her that Mma Botumile knew, and that Mma Botumile was not the sort of woman who would countenance her husband's having an affair. A sensible girlfriend would then understand that a choice had to be made. She could fight for Mr Botumile and prise him away from his wife, or she could find another man. What she could not do was to continue to be a rival to Mma Botumile while her husband was still with her.

It was almost on impulse that Mr J.L.B. Matekoni went into the office to ask Mma Makutsi if he could borrow the agency camera. This camera had been bought at an early stage in the existence of the No. 1 Ladies' Detective Agency, in the belief that it would be necessary for the obtaining of evidence. Clovis Andersen had advised this, saying that *while one cannot say that a camera never lies, it is hard to beat photographic evidence. Many is the time that I have personally confronted a malefactor with a photograph of himself engaged in something discreditable and said, 'There, who's that then? The Man in the Moon?'* It was Mma Makutsi who had read this passage, been impressed, and suggested the purchase of the camera. She had hardly ever used it but the camera, ready and loaded with film, sat on a shelf behind Mma Ramotswe's desk, awaiting its moment.

Armed with the camera, Mr J.L.B. Matekoni had then left the garage, instructions having been given to the younger apprentice to lock up, and had driven in his truck to exactly that spot outside the office building where he had previously waited for Mr Botumile. He had been in position for ten minutes by the time that the front door opened and a man came out and headed for one of the two red cars parked to the side of the building. Although he was the first man out after five, this was not Mr Botumile, but the other man, and Mr J.L.B. Matekoni ignored him as he got into the car and drove away. Then, a few minutes later, Mr Botumile appeared and climbed into his car.

Mr J.L.B. Matekoni followed the red car. The traffic was light, for some reason, and it was easy to keep a reasonable distance back without losing sight of his quarry. This time a new route was followed, and the red car drove back towards the Tlokweng Road. The main road was, of course, much busier, and he had to be careful not to lose sight of Mr Botumile's car, but he was close enough, and alert enough, not to miss it as it turned sharply off to the right a short distance after the shopping centre. Mr J.L.B. Matekoni was fairly familiar with the dirt road down which the red vehicle now travelled. This was not far from the garage and he occasionally drove down here to test a car that he had repaired, especially if new suspension needed to be tried out. It was mostly a residential area, sparsely populated, although there were one or two business plots at the Tlokweng Road end. It was also a road for goats, he remembered, as a bit of land halfway down was given over to these destructive creatures. It had been stripped almost bare of vegetation, apart from a few thorn bushes which had defeated even the talents of the goats. Now, as he drove down it, following the small cloud of dust thrown up from the wheels of Mr Botumile's car, he saw a few goats standing by the side of the road, nibbling at a piece of sacking which had been blown against a fence. These were odd parts of the town; not quite the bush, which was just beyond the fences, but heading that way, prone to the incursions of animals.

Suddenly the rear lights of Mr Botumile's car glowed through the dust and he swung into the driveway of a house. Mr J.L.B. Matekoni, reacting quickly, slowed down and then drew in to the side of the road. He would wait a minute or so, he thought, before he drove past the house. This would give Mr Botumile time to get out of the car, if he was going to get out, or pick up his waiting girlfriend, if that was what he had in mind.

By the time he drove past, Mr Botumile was out of his car. Mr J.L.B. Matekoni saw him walking up a short path towards the door of the house. He saw the door open, and he saw a woman standing there, waiting. It was not much more than a brief glimpse, but it was etched indelibly in his mind— the man, his lover, the dispirited dust-covered vegetation in the yard of the house, the angle of the gate, which was off its hinge, the stand-pipe at the side of the house. Was this what a clandestine affair looked like?

He went further down the road until he came to a place where he could turn without being seen from the house. Then he drove back slowly, this time with the camera ready on his lap. As he drew level with the house, he slowed down slightly, and, manipulating the camera with one hand while the other hand was on the steering wheel, he took a photograph of the house. Then, his heart beating

140

hard with the sheer excitement of it, he accelerated back in the direction of the Tlokweng Road. He felt confused. It had been an exhilarating experience in one sense, and he had felt the satisfaction of seeing what he had expected to see. But the act of taking the photograph seemed to him to have been an intrusion of a quite different degree from that of following Mr Botumile. He glanced down at the camera beside him on the seat of the truck; the sight of it, with its prying lens, made him feel dirty. This was not like being a mechanic; this was like being . . . well, it was like being a spy, an informant, a seeker-out of the tawdry secrets of others.

He thought that he would discuss it with Mma Ramotswe. It was impossible to imagine her ever doing anything that was wrong or shabby, and if she said that in this case the end justified the means, then he would be satisfied. But then he thought again: the whole point about this investigation was that he was doing it himself; he should not run off to Mma Ramotswe the moment anything difficult arose. No, he would have the film developed and he would show the photograph to Mma Botumile. But first he would find out who lived in that house so that he might reveal to her the chapter and verse of her husband's infidelity. He did not envy Mr Botumile after that, but then it was really not for him, Mr J.L.B. Matekoni, to pass judgement on a client's marriage, other than to come to the conclusion, privately, that if Mma Botumile were the last woman in Botswana and he were the last man, he would stay resolutely single.

* * *

141

While Mr J.L.B. Matekoni wrestled with his conscience, Mma Makutsi was preparing a meal for Phuti Radiphuti in her house in Extension Two. The previous evening had been one of his days to eat at his aunt's house, and this meant that he would be looking forward to Mma Makutsi's cooking. Mma Makutsi cooked what Phuti Radiphuti wanted, whereas his aunt cooked what she thought he should eat. That evening, she had prepared fried chicken with rice into which sultanas had been sprinkled. There was also fried banana, which always seemed to go so well with chicken, and a small jar of Mozambiquan peri-peri sauce which gave a kick to everything. Phuti Radiphuti had revealed a taste for hot food, which Mma Makutsi was trying to acquire herself. She was making some progress in that, but it was slow, and frequent glasses of water were required.

Their conversation ranged over the events of the past few days. Mma Makutsi had debated with herself whether to reveal her abortive resignation, and had eventually decided that she would do so. She did not come out of the episode very well, she thought, but she had never concealed anything from him, and she did not want to start doing so now.

'I made a fool of myself yesterday,' she said to him, as she stirred the fried chicken in the pan. 'I thought I would go and get another job.' That was all she said. She had thought that she would tell him everything, but now, in the end, she did not. There was no mention of the encounter with Violet and of the humiliation that had entailed; there was no mention of the broken shoe, nor of the ignominious barefoot walk, nor the thorn.

She was surprised by the strength of his reaction to the news. 'But you can't do that!' he exploded. 'What about Mma Ramotswe! You can't leave Mma Ramotswe!'

Taken aback, Mma Makutsi made an attempt to defend herself. 'But there's my career to think about,' she protested. 'What about me?'

Phuti Radiphuti seemed unmoved. 'What would Mma Ramotswe do without you?' he asked. 'You are the one who knows where everything is. You have done all the filing. You know all the clients. You cannot leave Mma Ramotswe.'

Mma Makutsi listened to this with foreboding. It seemed to her that he cared more about Mma Ramotswe than he did about her. Surely as her fiancé he should side with her in all this, should have her interests at heart rather than those of Mma Ramotswe, worthy though she undoubtedly was?

'I came back very quickly,' she said lamely. 'I was only away for the morning.'

Phuti Radiphuti looked at her with concern. 'Mma Ramotswe relies on you, Mma,' he said. 'You know that?'

Mma Makutsi replied that she did. But there were times when one had to move on, did he not think . . .

She did not finish. 'And I can understand why she cannot do without you,' Phuti continued. 'It is the same reason why I cannot do without you.'

Mma Makutsi was silent.

Phuti reached for the bottle of peri-peri sauce and fiddled with the cap as he spoke. 'It is because you are such a fine person,' he said. 'That is why.'

143

Mma Makutsi gave the chicken a final stir and then sat down. What had begun as a reproach had turned, it seemed, into a compliment. And she could not remember when she had last been complimented for anything; she had forgotten Mma Ramotswe's complimentary remark about her red dress.

'That's very kind, Phuti,' she said.

Phuti put down the bottle of sauce and began to fish for something in the pocket of his jacket. 'I am not one to make a speech,' he said.

'But you are getting better at it,' said Mma Makutsi. Which was true, she thought; that dreadful stammer had been more or less banished since she had met him, even if it manifested itself now and then when he became flustered. But that was all part of his charm; the charm of this man, her fiancé, the man who would become her husband.

'I am not one to make a speech,' Phuti repeated. 'But there is something that I have for you here which I want to give you. It is a ring, Mma. It is a diamond. I have bought it for you.'

He slipped a box across the table to Mma Makutsi. She took it with fumbling hands and prised it open there on the table. The diamond caught the light.

'It is one of our diamonds,' he said. 'It is a Botswana diamond.'

Mma Makutsi was silent as she took the ring from the box and fitted it onto her finger. She looked at Phuti and began to say something, but stopped. It was hard to find the words; that she who had been given so little, should now get this; that this gift, beyond her wildest yearnings, should

144

come from him; how could she express what she felt?

'One of our diamonds?'

'Yes. It is from our land.'

She pressed the ring, and the stone, to her cheek. It was cold to the touch; so precious; so pure.

CHAPTER THIRTEEN

The Good Impression Printing Works

Everybody, apart from Mr Polopetsi, and the younger apprentice of course, now had something to investigate. They approached this task with differing degrees of enthusiasm—Mr J.L.B. Matekoni, who believed that his investigation was almost over, felt buoyant. He now had photographic evidence—or at least one photograph of Mr Botumile's love nest—and all he had to do now was to find the name of the person who lived there. That was a simple enquiry which would not take long, and armed with the answer he could go to Mma Botumile and give her the information she needed. That would undoubtedly please her, but, more than that, it would impress Mma Ramotswe, who would be surprised at the speed with which he had managed to bring the enquiry to a satisfactory conclusion. The exposed film had been deposited at the chemist for developing and would be ready later that morning; there was no reason, then, why he should not see Mma Botumile the following day. To this end he telephoned her and asked if she would care to come to the office at any time convenient to her. He might have expected a snippy response even to that simple invitation. And that is what he got: no time, she said, was convenient. 'I am an extremely busy woman,' she snapped. 'But you can call on me, maybe I will be in, maybe not.'

Mr J.L.B. Matekoni sighed as he replaced the receiver. There were some people, it seemed, who were incapable of being pleasant about anything; that was what they were like when it came to the mending of their cars, and that was what they were like in relation to everything. Of course, the cars that such people drove tended to be difficult as well, now that he came to think about it. Nice cars have nice drivers; bad cars have bad drivers. A person's gearbox revealed everything that you could want to know about that person, thought Mr J.L.B. Matekoni.

He wondered whether Mr Botumile had been aware of his wife's irascible nature before he had asked her to marry him. *If* he had ever proposed marriage; it may well have been the other way round. Sometimes men cannot remember the circumstances in which they asked their wives to marry them, for the very good reason that no identifiable proposal was ever made. These are the men, thought Mr J.L.B. Matekoni, who are trapped into matrimony, who drift into it, who are eventually cornered by feminine wiles and find that a date has been set. In his own case he remembered very well the circumstances in which he had asked Mma Ramotswe to be his wife, but the memory of the way in which the day was actually selected was very much hazier. He had

146

been at the orphan farm, he believed, and Mma Potokwani had said something about how important it was for a woman to know when a wedding would be—something like that—and then the next thing he knew was that he was standing under that big tree and Trevor Mwamba was conducting the wedding service.

Mr J.L.B. Matekoni, of course, was very content being the husband of Mma Ramotswe, and he would never conceive of a situation in which he would be unhappy with her. But how different it must be—and what a nightmare—to discover that the person whom one has married is somebody one just does not like. People did make such a discovery, sometimes only a week or two into the marriage, and it must be a bleak one. Mr J.L.B. Matekoni knew that you were supposed to make an effort with your marriage, that you should at least try to get on with your spouse, but what if you found that she was somebody like Mma Botumile? He shuddered at the thought. Poor Mr Botumile having to listen to that shrill, complaining voice every day, no doubt running him down, criticising his every move, his every remark, making a prison for him, a prison of put-downs and belittlements. There but for the grace of God, he thought, go I. This feeling for Mr Botumile, this sympathy, was the only drawback in the way he felt about the whole enquiry. And even then, in spite of his understanding of Mr Botumile's plight, he was proud of the fact that he had been able to be so professional about the whole matter. He had sympathised with the husband in this case, but he had not let it obscure the fact that he was working for the wife.

For Mma Makutsi, the investigation of Teenie's problem with her dishonest employee was less clear-cut. It might well be that one of the employees at the printing works looked shifty, but she very much doubted that his shifty looks alone meant that he was the thief. He might be, of course, and she would keep an open mind on that, but she could certainly not allow her investigation to be skewed by any presumption of guilt. Or that, at least, is what she told herself as she paid off the taxi that she had hired to take her from the agency office to the premises of Teenie's printing company. Thirty pula! She tucked the receipt carefully into the pocket of her cardigan; it would have cost two pula, at the most, to make the journey by minibus, but the exorbitant cost of the taxi could properly be passed on to the client and, anyway, she told herself, it would be quite inappropriate for her to arrive at the printing works in a battered and over-loaded vehicle, complete with hands and feet sticking out of the windows. People noted how people travelled, and if she was going to pass herself off as a potential client of the company, then she should arrive in fitting style. Clovis Andersen probably said something about this in *The Principles of Private Detection*, but even if he did not, common sense dictated it.

The Good Impression Printing Company occupied half of a largish building in the industrial site that lay beyond the diamond-sorting building. It was not a very impressive building—one of those structures that look like cheap warehouses and which have few windows. Above their door was a sign saying *Words mean business. Business means money. Make a good impression with the Good Impression Printing Company!* And below that was a picture of a glossy brochure out of which, as from a cornucopia, banknotes cascaded. It was a powerful message, thought Mma Makutsi, and it made her think that perhaps it was time to speak to Mma Ramotswe about a new sign for the agency. That might also have an illustration of some sort to brighten the signboard, but what might it be? A tea-pot was the image that most immediately sprang to mind, but that would hardly do: there was no particular association in the public mind between private detection and tea, even if tea-drinking was an important part of their day's activities. Mma Ramotswe drank six cups a day—at the office; she had no idea how much bush tea was consumed at home—and she herself drank four, or perhaps five, if one counted the occasional top-up. But this was no time to think about such things, she decided; this was a delicate enquiry, conducted *under cover*, and she would have to think herself into the part she was about to play—a client inspecting a potential supplier.

Mma Makutsi entered a reception area at the front of the building. It was not a large room and the receptionist's desk dominated the available space, leaving only a cramped corner for a few chairs. Beside these chairs was a small table on which paper samples and some trade magazines had been stacked.

There was a curious smell in the air, an almost acrid smell that took her a moment to recognise as the smell of ink. That took her back, to the school in Bobonong, where they had a room with a duplicating machine and supplies of the ink that it

149

used. It was an old machine of the sort that nobody used any more, and it had been forgotten by the authorities, but the school kept it going. The children had helped with the task of duplication, and she had watched in wonder as the newly printed pages emerged from beneath the circulating drum. And now, a world away from that place and those days, she remembered the smell of ink.

She gave her name to the receptionist, who telephoned and called through to Teenie Magama. Then she sat down on one of the chairs in the corner and waited until Teenie arrived.

She looked at the receptionist, a middle-aged woman wearing what looked like a housecoat but which she decided was actually a loose-fitting dress. Her outfit was far from smart, and Mma Makutsi found herself thinking, *It's not her. This woman has no spare cash. If she were stealing, then one would expect . . . Or would one? Desperation drove people to theft, did it not?* She looked at her more closely.

She decided on a general question. If you could think of nothing to say to somebody, you could always ask them how long they had been doing whatever it was that they were doing. People always seemed willing to talk about that. 'Have you worked here very long, Mma?' Mma Makutsi asked.

The receptionist, who had been typing, looked up from her keyboard.

'I do not belong to this place,' she said. 'I am here because my daughter is sick. She is the one who has this job. I am standing in for her.' She paused. 'And I do not know what I am doing, Mma.

150

I am just sitting here, but I do not know what I am doing.'

Mma Makutsi laughed, but the woman shook her head. 'No, I am serious, Mma. I really don't know what I'm doing. I try to answer the phone, but I end up cutting people off. And I do not know the names of any of the people in the works back there. Except for Mma Magama herself. That Teenie person. I know her name.'

'There are many people who do not know what they are doing,' said Mma Makutsi. 'It is not unusual. In fact, maybe even most people do not know. They pretend to know, but they do not really know.'

The receptionist smiled. 'Then I am not alone, Mma.'

Mma Makutsi tried another tack. 'Is your daughter happy here?' she asked.

The woman's answer came quickly. 'Very happy. She is very happy, Mma. She is always telling other people what a good boss she has. Not everybody can say that.'

Mma Makutsi was about to say that she could, but stopped herself in time. She could not tell this woman about Mma Ramotswe because that would give away what she did and she was meant to be a prospective client, not a private detective. So she said nothing, and they drifted back into silence.

A few minutes later, Teenie appeared through a door behind the receptionist's desk. She was more plainly dressed than she had been when she had come to Mma Makutsi's office, and for a moment Mma Makutsi did not recognise her.

'Yes,' said Teenie. 'I am not looking smart now. These are my working clothes. And look, see what

151

my hands look like. Ink!'

Mma Makutsi rose to her feet and examined Teenie's outstretched hands. 'If I were a detective,' she said as she saw the large ink stains, like continents, on Teenie's upturned palms, 'I would say that you are a printer.' Then she added hurriedly, glancing down at the receptionist as she spoke, 'But I am not a detective, of course!'

'No, of course not,' said Teenie. 'You are not a detective, Mma.'

The receptionist, who had been following the conversation between the two of them, looked up sharply. 'You are a policewoman, Mma?'

Mma Makutsi noticed the concern in the woman's voice. 'I am nothing to do with the police,' she said. 'Nothing at all. I am a businesswoman.'

The receptionist relaxed visibly. Her sharp reaction, thought Mma Makutsi, was unusual. She clearly had something to hide, but it was probably nothing to do with her daughter or the job at the printing works. Unless, of course, she knew that her daughter had been stealing from the works. Mothers and daughters can be close; they tell each other things, and the knowledge that one's daughter was a thief would obviously make one dread the arrival of the police. But then she reminded herself that there were plenty of people who were afraid of the police, even if they had clear consciences. These were people who had been the victims of bullying when young—bullying by severe teachers, by stronger children; there were so many ways in which people could be crushed. Such people might fear the police in the same way in which they feared all authority.

152

Mma Makutsi smiled at the receptionist and followed Teenie through the door into the works. The other woman was so small that even though Mma Makutsi was herself only of average height, she found herself looking down on the top of Teenie's head; at a small woollen bobble, in fact, which topped a curious tea-cosy style knitted cap which she was wearing. She looked more closely at it, wondering if she could make out an opening through which a tea-pot spout might project; she could not see an opening, but there was a very similar tea-cosy in the office, she remembered, and perhaps she or Mma Ramotswe might wear it on really cold days. She imagined how Mma Ramotswe would look in a tea-cosy and decided that she would probably look rather good; it might add to her authority, perhaps, in some indefinable way.

On the other side of the door was a short corridor. The smell she had picked up when she first came into the building was stronger now, and there was noise too, the obedient clatter of a machine performing some repetitive task. From the background somewhere, there came strains of radio music.

'Our new machine is on,' said Teenie proudly. 'That is it making that noise. Listen. That is our new German machine printing a brochure. They make very good machines, the Germans, you know, Mma.'

Mma Makutsi agreed. 'Yes,' she said. 'They do. They are . . .' She was not sure how to continue. She had been about to pass a further comment on the Germans, but realised that she actually knew very little about them. The Chinese one saw a lot

153

of, and they seemed quiet and industrious too, but one did not see many Germans. In fact, she had seen none.

Teenie turned and looked up at her. The expectant, plaintive look was there; as if there was something important that Mma Makutsi might say about the Germans and which she desperately wanted to hear.

'I would like to go to Germany,' said Mma Makutsi, lamely.

'Yes,' said Teenie. 'I would like to visit other countries. I would like to go to London some day. But I do not think I shall ever get out of Botswana. This business keeps me tied up. It is like a chain around my ankle sometimes. You cannot go anywhere if you have a chain around your ankle.'

'No,' said Mma Makutsi, raising her voice now to compete with the sound of the German printing machine.

Mma Makutsi gazed about her. If she needed to act the part of the interested client, then it was not a difficult role for her to fill; she was very interested. They were in a large, high-ceilinged space, windowless but with an open door at the back. The sun streamed through the back door, but the main lighting was provided by a bank of fluorescent tube lights hanging from the ceiling. In the centre of the room stood the German printing machine, while four or five other complicated-looking machines were arranged around the rest of the area. Mma Makutsi noticed an electric guillotine, with shavings of paper below, and large bottles of what must have been ink on high racked shelves. There were several large supply cupboards, walk-in affairs, and stacks of supplies

154

on trolleys and tables. It was a good place for a thief, she thought; there were plenty of *things*.

Next, she noticed the people. There were two young men standing at the side of the German printing machine: one engaged in some sort of adjusting task, the other watching a rapidly growing pile of printed brochures. At the far end of the room, two women were stacking piles of paper onto a trolley, while a third person, a man, was doing something to what looked like another, smaller printing machine. Just off the main space there were two blocked-off glass cubicles, small offices. One was empty, but lit; a man and a woman were in the other, the woman showing a piece of paper to a man. When Mma Makutsi looked in their direction, the woman nudged the man and pointed at her. The man looked across the room.

'You should introduce me to the staff,' said Mma Makutsi. 'Why don't we start with those two?' She indicated the two young men attending to the large printing machine.

'They are very nice young men,' said Teenie. 'They are my best people. They have a printer's eye, Mma. Do you know what a printer's eye is? It means that they can see how things are going to turn out even before the machine is turned on.'

Mma Makutsi thought of the two apprentices. If there was such a thing as a mechanic's eye, then she doubted whether the apprentices had it.

'Printers used to be able to read backwards,' said Teenie as they approached the machine and its two young attendants. 'They could do that when type was set in metal. They put the letters in backwards.'

'Mirrors,' said Mma Makutsi. 'They must have had mirrors in their heads.'

'No,' said Teenie. 'They did not.'

As they approached the printing machine, the two young men stopped what they were doing. One flicked a switch and the machine ground to a halt. Without the noise it had been making the works now seemed unnaturally quiet, apart from the radio in the background somewhere which could still be heard churning out the insistent beat of a rock tune, the sort of music that Mma Ramotswe described as the sound of an angry stomach.

The young men were dressed in work overalls and one of them now took a cloth out of his pocket and wiped his hands on it. The other, who had a large mouth, which he kept open, reached a finger up to fiddle with his nose, but thought better of it and dropped his hand to his side.

'This lady is a client,' said Teenie. 'She is very interested in printing. You could tell her about the new machine. She is called Mma Makutsi.'

Mma Makutsi smiled encouragingly at the young men. She tried to keep her eyes off the face of the young man with the gaping mouth, but found that she could not; such a deep space, like the mouth of a cave, allowing one to see straight into his head. It was fascinating, in a curious, uncomfortable way.

The printer who had wiped his hands on the cloth leaned forward to shake hands with Mma Makutsi. He spoke politely to her, and told her his name. While this was happening, Mma Makutsi felt the eyes of the other young man on her. She glanced at him, but saw only the open mouth. Absurdly, temptingly, she wanted to put something into it: pieces of paper, perhaps, small erasers, anything that would block it up; it was ridiculous.

Then the young man spoke. 'You are that lady from the detective agency,' he said. 'That place on the Tlokweng Road.' The sound of his voice may have come from his mouth, but to Mma Makutsi it seemed that it really came from somewhere below, down in his chest or stomach.

Mma Makutsi looked at Teenie, who turned to stare up at her in blank surprise. 'I am that lady,' she stuttered. 'Yes.'

There was silence. Mma Makutsi was momentarily at a loss as to what to say. She felt an intense irritation that this young man, with his disconcerting mouth, should expose her so quickly. But then she began to wonder how he knew. It was flattering to think that she was well known, a public figure almost, even if it meant that she would be unable to carry out enquiries quite as discreetly as she hoped; certainly this enquiry was ruined now, as everybody here would know within minutes who she was.

Her surprise turned to anger. 'So I am that lady,' she snapped at the young man. 'But that means nothing. Nothing at all.'

'I've never met a detective,' said the young man with the cloth. 'Is it interesting work, Mma? Do you come to places like this to investigate . . .'

'Thefts,' supplied the mouth.

Teenie gave a start. She had been watching the young men as they talked; now she spun round and looked at Mma Makutsi. Again there was that pleading look, as if she wanted Mma Makutsi to say that it was not true, that she was not a detective, and that she had certainly not come here to look into thefts.

157

Mma Makutsi decided that the best tactic would be to pretend to be amused by the very suggestion. 'We do not spend all our time investigating,' she said, smiling archly. 'There are other things in our lives.'

The young man with the large mouth cocked his head sideways as she spoke, as if he was trying to look at Mma Makutsi from a different angle. She glanced at him and found herself looking past his teeth and lips, into the very cave, the labyrinth. There were people who found such caves irresistible, she knew, who loved exploring. She imagined tiny people, equipped with minuscule ropes and picks, climbing into that mouth, leaning into the hot gusts of wind that came up from the lungs somewhere down below.

Teenie took Mma Makutsi's arm and led her off towards the offices. 'They are not involved in it,' she said. 'They would never steal.'

Mma Makutsi was not so sure. 'One can't be too sure about that,' she said. 'Sometimes it is the most unlikely person who is to blame for something. We have had many cases where you would never have suspected the person who turns out to be guilty. Ministers of religion for example. Yes. Even them.'

'I cannot imagine a minister of religion doing anything bad,' said Teenie.

Mma Makutsi sighed. 'Well, they do. There are some very wicked ministers of religion. They hardly ever get caught, of course, because nobody thinks of looking into their affairs. If I wanted to commit a crime and get away with it, you know what I would do? I would become a minister of religion first, and then I would commit the crime. I would know that I would get away with it, you see.'

'Or a detective,' said Teenie quietly.

'Or a . . .' Mma Makutsi had been about to agree with this, but was stopped by professional pride. 'No,' she continued. 'I don't think that it would be a good idea to become a detective if you were planning to commit a crime. The people you worked with would know, you see, Mma. They would just know.'

Teenie said nothing. They were now outside the office cubicle and Teenie was reaching for the handle of the door. The man and the woman inside were watching them.

'This is him,' whispered Teenie. 'This one inside.'

Mma Makutsi looked in through the glass wall. Her eyes met the gaze of the man in the office. Of course, she thought. Now I see.

CHAPTER FOURTEEN

Charlie Picks up a Passenger

The taxi licence for which Charlie had applied would be approved, he had been told, but the document itself, the important piece of paper, would not be ready for at least two weeks. For a young man of Charlie's age, and attitude, that was a long time—too long a time to wait for a mere bureaucratic formality. And so he had decided to start plying his trade rather than wait for the officials in the public transport department to get round to picking up their rubber stamps and validating his papers. Those idle civil servants! he

159

thought. There are too many of them in this country. That is all that we make—civil servants. He smiled. He was a businessman now—he could think such thoughts.

The car which he had acquired from Mr J.L.B. Matekoni had been cleaned and polished until it shone. Charlie lived as a lodger with a maternal uncle, who had a small two-room house at the side of a busy street off the Francistown Road. The now gleaming Mercedes-Benz looked out of place among the shabby cars that stood outside these modest houses and Charlie was worried that it would be stolen. On the first night that the car spent in its new quarters, Charlie had decided to tie a piece of string to the front grille of the vehicle and then feed the other end of the string through the window of the room in which he slept. That would then be tied to his big toe before he got into bed.

'You will certainly wake up if the car is stolen,' said his uncle, who had watched, bemused, as the string was unwound from its ball.

'That is why I am doing it, Uncle,' Charlie had replied. 'If I wake up when the car is moved, I can get out of bed and deal with the thieves.'

The uncle had stared at his nephew. 'There are two problems that I see,' he said. 'Two. The first is this: what if the string does not break? This new string is very strong, you know. I think it could probably take the weight of a man. It could pull your toe out of the window, with you still attached.'

Charlie said nothing. He stared down at the ball of string. The label proclaimed: *Extra Strong*.

'Then there is another problem,' said the uncle. 'Even if the string woke you up and then broke

160

before it pulled your toe off, what would happen then? How exactly are you going to deal with your car being driven away? Run after it?'

Charlie put the ball of string down on the table. 'Maybe I will not do this,' he said.

'No,' said the uncle. 'Maybe you shouldn't.'

The car was not stolen that night. When Charlie awoke the next morning, he immediately rose from his mattress on the floor and pulled aside the thin cotton curtain that covered his window. The car was still there, exactly where he had left it, and he breathed a sigh of relief.

That morning he had arranged for a sign-painter to stencil the name of his taxi firm on the driver's door. This took barely an hour to do, but consumed almost half of the final week's pay that Mr J.L.B. Matekoni had given him. At least he would not have to pay for fuel just yet, as Mr J.L.B. Matekoni had given him a full tank of petrol as a parting gift. So now he was ready, apart from the licence.

Charlie stood outside the sign-painter's shop and admired the newly painted legend on the side of the car.

The sign-painter, a cigarette hanging out of the side of his mouth, contemplated his handiwork. 'Why are you calling it the No. 1 Ladies' Taxi Service?' he asked. 'Are you getting a lady driver?'

Charlie explained the nature of the service to the painter, an explanation which was followed by a brief silence. Then the painter said, 'There are some very good business ideas, Rra. In my job, I see many businesses starting. But I hardly ever see one which is as good an idea as this.'

'Do you mean that?' asked Charlie.

161

'Of course. This is going to be a big success, I can tell you, Rra. A big success. You are going to be very rich. Next month, maybe the month after that, you will be starting to get rich. You'll see. You come back and tell me if I'm wrong.'

Charlie drove away with the sign-painter's prediction ringing in his ears. Of course the thought of being rich appealed to him; apart from that brief spell when he had been taken up by that wealthy, married and older woman, he had known only poverty so far, had owned only a single pair of shoes, had made do with turned collars on his shirts. If he had the money, he could dress in a way which he knew would attract the girls; not that he had ever had any difficulty in doing that, but in a way which would attract a fancier sort of girl. That was what interested him.

He had intended to drive straight home in order to conserve fuel, but then, as he rounded a corner, a woman stepped out from a driveway and waved him down. For a moment he was puzzled, and then he remembered. *I am a taxi driver! I get waved down.*

He drew in at the side of the road, coming to rest immediately abreast of the woman. She stepped smartly to the back door and climbed in. He watched her in his rear-view mirror; a well-off woman, he thought; well-dressed, carrying a small leather briefcase.

'Where to?' he asked. He had not rehearsed the phrase, but it sounded right.

She told him that she wanted to go to the bank at the top of the Mall. 'I have an appointment,' she said. 'I am a bit late for it. I hope that you can get me there quickly.'

He shifted the car into gear and drove off. 'I will do my best, Mma.'

In the mirror he saw the woman in the back relax. 'A friend was coming to collect me,' she said, looking out of the window as she spoke. 'She has obviously forgotten. It was a good thing you came along.'

'Yes, Mma. We are here to help.'

The woman seemed impressed with this. 'Some of you taxi people are really rude,' she said. 'You are not like that. That is a good thing.'

Charlie looked in the mirror again, his eyes meeting his passenger's gaze. She was a good-looking woman, he thought; a bit too old for him, but one never knew. That last time, when he had been involved with that older woman, he had enjoyed a marvellous time, until her husband . . . Well, one could never tell how these things would work out. He glanced into the mirror once more. She was wearing a necklace with green stones and a pair of large dangling ear-rings. Charlie liked ear-rings like that. They were a sign that a woman liked a good time, he always thought. Perhaps he might ask this woman at the end of the journey whether he could come back and pick her up after her appointment. And she would say to him that this would be a very good idea because, as it happened, she had nothing to do and perhaps they could go out to a bar somewhere and have a beer because it was getting hot again, did he not think, and it would be a good thing to say goodbye to these winter nights when one really needed somebody nice and warm in one's bed to keep the chill away . . .

He did not see the traffic lights, which were red,

163

against him; nor the truck that was approaching and that had no time to apply its brakes. Charlie, gazing in his rear-view mirror, saw nothing that lay ahead; not the frantic movements of the truck driver as he realised that impact was inevitable; not the crumpling of metal as the front of the car folded in; not the shattering of the windscreen as it fragmented into little pieces, like diamonds or droplets of water in the sun. But he heard the screaming of the woman in the seat behind him and a slow ticking sound from the engine of his car; he heard the slamming of the door of the truck as the driver, shaking, let himself out of his relatively unharmed cabin. He heard the protests of metal as his own door was prised open.

Another motorist had stopped and had put his arm around Charlie's passenger. She was standing beside the car, weeping with shock. There was no blood.

'Everybody is all right,' said the other motorist. 'I saw it happen. I saw it.'

'I was coming that way,' stuttered the truck driver. 'The light was green.'

'Yes,' said the motorist. 'I saw that. The light was green.'

They looked at Charlie. 'Are you all right, Rra? You are not injured?'

Charlie could not speak. He shook his head. He had escaped injury, thanks to the solidity of German engineering.

'God must be watching,' said a passer-by, who had seen all three step unharmed from the wreckage. 'But look at that car! I'm sorry, Rra. Your poor car.'

Charlie had now sat down on the side of the

road. He, too, was shaking. He was staring at his shoes; now he looked up and saw the ruins of his Mercedes-Benz, with its crumpled front, stained green by spurting coolant; at the metal rubbed bare where the truck had ground across it; at the buckled door with its newly painted sign. The ruptured metal had shortened the sign. *The No. 1 Ladies' Tax* it now read; a curious legend which caused the policeman who shortly afterwards arrived at the scene to scratch his head. Tax?

Charlie reached home four hours later. His aunt was there, and she could tell immediately that there was something wrong.

'I have had an accident,' he said.

The aunt let out a wail. 'Your beautiful new car?'

'It is finished, Aunty. That car is finished now.'

The aunt looked fixedly at the ground; she had known, of course, that this, or something like this, would happen. Charlie, silent now that he had pronounced the requiem on his car, sat down. I am twenty, he thought. Twenty, and it is all finished for me.

CHAPTER FIFTEEN

Mma Potokwani on the Subject of Trust, amongst Other Things

On the day following Charlie's accident—an accident of which nobody at the garage or the agency was yet aware—Mma Ramotswe decided not to work in her office but instead to go for a picnic. It was not a decision that was made on the

165

spur of the moment; she had been invited almost two weeks previously by Mma Potokwani, had accepted, and then forgotten about it until a few hours before the gathering was due to take place. In some respects she would have preferred not to have remembered at all, as that would have given her a perfect excuse, even if a retrospective one, for not attending. But now it was too late: Mma Potokwani, the redoubtable matron of the orphan farm, would be expecting her and she had to go.

Mma Ramotswe and Mma Potokwani were old friends. Mma Makutsi, who had her difficulties with Mma Potokwani, the two having crossed swords on more than one occasion, had once asked Mma Ramotswe how they had first met. Mma Ramotswe had been unable to provide an answer. Some friends, she explained, seemed always to have been part of one's life. Obviously there was a first meeting, but in the case of old friends that was usually so long ago, and so mundane at the time, that all memory of it had faded. Such friends were like favoured possessions—a cherished book, a favourite picture—how one acquired them was long forgotten, they were just there.

It had not always been the smoothest of friendships and there were some aspects of Mma Potokwani's behaviour of which Mma Ramotswe frankly disapproved. Her bossiness was one such thing, particularly when it was directed at Mr J.L.B. Matekoni, who had long been incapable of refusing Mma Potokwani's requests to fix various antiquated pieces of equipment at the orphan farm. It was all very well for her to order the orphans about—that was what one expected of the matron of an orphanage, since it was undoubtedly good for the children to lead ordered lives—but it was another thing altogether for her to adopt a similar manner when it came to adults.

'I feel sorry for that woman's husband,' Mma Makutsi had once remarked, following upon a call that Mma Potokwani had made to the office. 'No wonder he doesn't ever say anything. Have you watched him? He just stands there. The poor man must be afraid to open his mouth.'

Out of loyalty to her friend, Mma Ramotswe refrained from saying anything about this, but when she gave some thought to Mma Makutsi's less-than-charitable remark she had to acknowledge that it was probably true. Mma Potokwani's husband was a small man, neither as tall nor as well built as his wife, and he gave every appearance of being both physically and emotionally floundering in the wake created by his wife.

'I wonder why he married her,' Mma Makutsi went on. 'Do you think that he asked her, or did she ask him?' She paused as she mulled over the possibilities. 'Maybe she even ordered him to marry her. Do you think that happened, Mma?'

Mma Ramotswe pursed her lips. It was difficult not to smile when Mma Makutsi got going on remarks like this, but she knew that she should not. It was none of Mma Makutsi's business how Rra Potokwani had proposed to Mma Potokwani; such things were the private business of man and wife and people had no right to pry into such areas. Mind you, Mma Makutsi might not be far wrong; she could just imagine Mma Potokwani instructing her mild, rather timid husband to marry her or face some unnamed unpleasant consequences.

'I wonder what their bed is like,' went on Mma Makutsi. 'I can just see their bedroom, can't you?—with her taking up most of the space on the bed and leaving only a few inches at the edge for him. Maybe he sleeps on the floor next to the bed. And then she wakes up and thinks: where on earth did I put my husband? Do you think that is what happens, Mma Ramotswe?'

This was overstepping the mark. Mma Ramotswe did not like to speculate on the bedrooms, or beds, of others. That was private. 'You mustn't talk like that,' she said. 'It is not funny.'

'But you are smiling,' Mma Makutsi said. 'I can see that you are trying not to smile, but you are.'

Mma Ramotswe had changed the subject at this point, but at home that evening she had narrated the conversation to Mr J.L.B. Matekoni and he had laughed. 'Those two just can't get on,' he said. 'They are really the same, under the skin. In ten years' time, Mma Makutsi will be just like her. She has been ordering the apprentices around—for practice. Soon she will move on to Mr Phuti Radiphuti. Once they are married, then the ordering about will begin.' He looked at Mma Ramotswe. 'Not all men are fools, you know, Mma. We know the plans that you women have for us.'

Oh, thought Mma Ramotswe, although she did not say oh. If Mr J.L.B. Matekoni thought that she had plans for him, then what exactly were they? There were undoubtedly women who had plans for their husbands; they were often ambitious for them in their jobs, and urged them to apply for promotion above the husbands of other women. Then there were women who liked their men to

168

have expensive cars, to be wealthy, to dress in flashy clothes. But she had no plans of that nature for Mr J.L.B. Matekoni. She did not want Tlokweng Road Speedy Motors to get any bigger or to make more money. Nor did she want Mr J.L.B. Matekoni to change in any way; she liked him exactly as he was, with his old, stained veldschoen, his overalls, his kind face, his gentle manner. No, if she had any plan for him it was that they would continue to live together in the house on Zebra Drive, that they would grow old in one another's company, and maybe one day go back to Mochudi and sit in the sun there, watching other people do things, but doing nothing themselves. Those were plans of a sort, she supposed, but surely they were plans that Mr J.L.B. Matekoni would himself endorse.

Now, driving her tiny white van along the road that led to the Gaborone dam, she let her thoughts wander: Mma Potokwani, men and their little ways, the Government, next year's rains, Motholeli's homework problems: there was so much to think about, even before she started to dwell upon any of her cases. Once she started to think about that side of her life, Mochudi Hospital came to mind, with its cool corridors, and the ward where three people had died, all in the same bed. Three fingers raised, one after the other, and then lowered. Three stitches taken out of our shared blanket. She had talked to how many people now? Four, if one did not count Tati Monyena, who was really the client, even if it was the hospital administration that was paying. Those four people, the three nurses and Dr Cronje, had all endorsed the view that Tati Monyena had voiced right at the beginning—that the deaths were just an extraordinary coincidence. But if that was what everybody believed, then why had they sought to involve her in the whole business? Perhaps it was one of those cases where doubts simply refused to lie down until somebody independent, somebody from the outside, had come and put them to rest. So she was not a detective, then, but a judge brought in to make a ruling, as judges, chiefs, will do when with a few carefully chosen words they bury a cause of conflict or doubt. If that were so, then there was not much for her to do but to declare that she had looked into the situation and found nothing suspicious.

And yet she was not sure if she could honestly say that. It was true that she had looked into the situation, and while she had been unable to come up with any idea as to why the patients had died, she could not truthfully say that she had no suspicions. In fact, she had felt quite uncomfortable after her conversations with the nurses and with Dr Cronje; she had sensed an awkwardness, an unhappiness. Of course, that could have been nothing to do with the matter she was investigating—Dr Cronje was an unhappy man because he was in self-imposed exile; and as for the nurses, for all she knew they might have some cause for resentment, some work issue, some unresolved humiliation that gnawed away; such things were common and could consume every waking moment of those who allowed them to do so.

She reached the point at which the public road, untarred and dusty, a track really, entered the confines of the dam area. Now the road turned to the east and followed the base of the dam wall until it swung round in the direction of the Notwane River and Otse beyond. It was a rough road, scraped flat now and then by the Water Department grader but given to potholes and corrugated ridges. She did not push the tiny white van on such roads, and stuck to a steady fifteen miles per hour, which would give her time to stop should she see too deep a hole in the road or should some wild animal dash out of cover and run across her path. And there were many animals here; she spotted a large kudu bull standing under an acacia tree, its horns spiralling up a good four feet. She saw duiker, too, and a family of warthogs scuttling off into the inadequate cover of the sparse thorn bush. There were dassies, rock hyrax, surprised in the open and running frantically for the shelter of their familiar rocks; as a girl, she had possessed a kaross made of the skins of these small creatures sewn together end to end, little patches of silky-smooth fur that had been draped across her sleeping mat and into which she had snuggled on cold nights. She wondered where that kaross was now; worn to the very leather, perhaps, abandoned, surviving as a few scraps of something, traces of a childhood which was so long ago.

Halfway along the dam, the road opened out onto a large clearing where somebody, a few years earlier, had tried to set up a public picnic ground. The attempt had been abandoned, but the signs of the effort were still there—a small breeze-block structure with *ladies* painted on one end and *gentlemen* on the other, the lettering still just discernible; now, with the roof off and half the walls down, the two sexes were jumbled up together in democratic ruin. And beyond that, over a token wall, now toppling over in places and never more than a couple of feet high, was a children's playground. The ants had eaten the wooden support posts of the swings and these had fallen and been encased in crumbling termite casts; a piece of flat metal, which could have been the surface of a slide, lay rusted in a clump of blackjack weeds; there was an old braaivleis site, now just a pile of broken bricks, picked clean by human scavengers of anything that could be used to make a shack somewhere.

Mma Ramotswe arrived half an hour early, and after she had found a shady spot for the van she decided to walk down to the edge of the water, some fifty yards away. It was very peaceful. Above her was an empty sky; endowed with so much room, so much light; on the other side of the dam, set back a bit, was Kgale Hill, rock upon rock. You could see the town on the other side of the wall, and you knew it was there, but if you turned your head the other way there was just Africa, or that bit of it, of acacia trees like small umbrellas, and dry grass, and red-brown earth, and termite mounds like miniature Babel towers. Paths led criss-cross to nowhere very much; paths created by the movement of game to the water, and she followed one of these down towards the edge of the dam. The water was light green, mirror flat, becoming blue in its further reaches. Reeds grew at its edge, not in clumps, but sparsely, individual needles projecting from the surface of the water.

Mma Ramotswe was cautious. There were crocodiles in the Notwane—everybody knew that—and they would be in the dam too, although some people denied it. But of course they would be here, because crocodiles could travel long distances over land, with that ungainly walk of theirs, seeking out fresh bodies of water. If they were in the Notwane, then they would be here too, waiting beneath the water, just at the edge, where an incautious warthog or duiker might venture. And then the crocodile would lunge out and seize its prey and drag it back into deeper water. And after that followed the roll, the twisting and churning, when the crocodile turned its prey round and round under water. That was how the end came, they said, if one was unfortunate enough to be taken by a crocodile.

There had been a bad crocodile attack at the end of the last rainy season, on the Limpopo, and Mma Ramotswe had discussed it with Mr J.L.B. Matekoni. He had known the victim, who was a friend of a cousin of his, a man who had a small farm up on the banks of the river and who had crossed the water in his boat to drive some cattle back. The cattle had somehow managed to cross the river to the wrong bank, onto somebody else's land, in spite of the fact that the water was high.

The Limpopo was not very wide at that point, but the central channel was deep, a place for a predator. The man was halfway across, seated in his boat with its small outboard motor, when a large crocodile had reared up out of the water and snatched him by the shoulder, dragging him into the river. The herd boy, who was with him in the boat, watched as it happened. At first he was not believed, as crocodiles very rarely attacked a boat, but he stuck to the story. They found what remained of the farmer eventually, and the herd boy was shown to be right.

She looked at the water. It was easy for a crocodile to conceal itself close to the edge, where there were rocks, clumps of half-submerged vegetation and lumps of mud breaking the surface. Any one of these could be the tip of a crocodile's snout, protruding from the water just enough to allow him to breathe; and, a short way away, two further tiny islands of mud were really his eyes, fixed on potential prey, watching. We are so used to being the predator, thought Mma Ramotswe. We are the ones to be feared, but here, at the edge of our natural element, were those who preyed on us.

Further out, a kingfisher hovered and then plummeted, stone-like, into the water; a splash of white spray, and then up again to a vantage point in the air. She watched this for a few moments, and smiled. Everything has its place, she thought; everything. And then she turned round and made her way slowly back up the track towards the van, to await the arrival of Mma Potokwani and the children. She thought she could hear an engine now, straining somewhere not too far away. That would be one of the orphan farm's minibuses, nursed and kept alive by Mr J.L.B. Matekoni, officially retired by Derek James, who ran the orphan farm office, and replaced with something newer, but brought back by Mma Potokwani, who could not bear to waste anything. The old minibuses were now used for work like this, since Mma Potokwani did not like the thought of the newer vehicles destroying their suspension on these bumpy roads.

There were two familiar old blue minibuses. The

174

first one, driven somewhat erratically by Mma Potokwani, drew up close to where Mma Ramotswe was standing and the matron herself got out. She opened the rear door and a chattering group of children spilled forth.

Mma Ramotswe made a quick mental count. There had been nineteen children in a vehicle made for twelve.

Mma Potokwani guessed Mma Ramotswe's thoughts. 'It was perfectly all right,' she said. 'Children are smaller. There's always room for one or two more children.' She turned and clapped her hands. 'Now, children, nobody is to go in the water. Play up here. Look, there used to be some swings over there. And a slide. So there's lots to do.'

'Be careful of crocodiles,' warned Mma Ramotswe. 'You don't want to be eaten.'

A small boy with wide eyes looked up at Mma Ramotswe. 'Would a crocodile eat me, Mma?' he asked politely. 'Even me?'

Mma Ramotswe smiled. Even me. None of us thinks that we will be eaten; no child thinks that he will die. 'Only if you weren't careful,' she said. 'Careful boys are never eaten by crocodiles. That is well known.' As she spoke, she realised that this was not true: that farmer had been careful. But children could not be told the unvarnished truth.

'I'll be careful, Mma.'

'Good.'

Mma Potokwani had brought two of the housemothers with them, as well as a couple of volunteers from Maru-a-Pula School. The children flocked round the teenage volunteers while the housemothers set out the picnic on small trestle tables. Mma Potokwani and Mma Ramotswe

175

found a small section of wall, shaded by a tree, and sat down on that.

Mma Potokwani drew a deep breath. 'I am always happy when I am in the bush,' she said. 'I think everybody is.'

'I certainly am,' said Mma Ramotswe. 'I live in a town, but I do not think my heart lives there.'

'Our stomachs live in towns,' said Mma Potokwani, patting the front of her dress. 'That is where the work is. Our stomachs know that. But our hearts are usually somewhere else.'

They were silent for a while. Above them, in the branches of the acacia, a small bird hopped from twig to twig. Mma Ramotswe watched the children exploring the abandoned playground. Two boys were kicking at the fallen swing posts, causing the dried mud of the termites' activity to puff up in little clouds of dust.

She pointed to the boys. 'Why do boys destroy things?'

Mma Potokwani sighed. 'That is just what they do,' she said. 'When I first started to work with children, years ago, I used to ask myself questions like that. But then I realised that there was no point. Boys are the way they are and girls are the way we are. You might as well ask why those dassies sit on the top of rocks. That's just the way they are.'

It was true, thought Mma Ramotswe. She liked doing the things that she liked doing, and Mr J.L.B. Matekoni was the same. She watched the children. 'They seem very happy,' she said.

'They are,' she said. 'Most of them have had a bad start. Now things are going well for them. They know that we love them. That is all they need to know.' She paused, and looked out over the water. 'In fact, Mma Ramotswe, that's really all that a child needs to know—to know that it is loved. That is all.'

Again, thought Mma Ramotswe, that was true.

'And if there's bad behaviour,' Mma Potokwani went on. 'If there's bad behaviour, the quickest way of stopping it is to give more love. That always works, you know. People say that we must punish when there is wrongdoing, but if you punish you're only punishing yourself. And what's the point of that?'

'Love,' mused Mma Ramotswe; such a small, powerful word.

Mma Potokwani's stomach grumbled. 'We must eat very soon. But, yes, love is the answer, Mma. Let me tell you about something that happened at the orphan farm. We had a child who was stealing from the food cupboard. Everybody knew that. The housemother in charge of that cupboard had seen the child do it. The other children knew.

'We talked to the child and told him that what he was doing was wrong. But still the stealing went on. And so we tried something different. We put a lock on the cupboard.'

Mma Ramotswe laughed. 'That seems reasonable enough, Mma.'

'You may laugh,' said Mma Potokwani. 'But then let me tell you what we did next. We gave the key to that child. All the children have little tasks that they must do. We put that boy in charge of the cupboard.'

'And?'

'And that stopped the stealing. Trust did it. We trusted him and he knew it. So he stopped stealing.

That was the end of the stealing.'

Mma Ramotswe was thinking. At the back of her mind there was something that she thought she might say to Mma Makutsi about this. But her thoughts were interrupted by one of the housemothers bringing them a large tin plate on which several pieces of fruit cake had been laid, along with a number of syrup sandwiches. The housemother handed the plate to Mma Ramotswe and went back to the children.

Mma Potokwani glanced at her friend. 'I think that is for both of us, Mma,' she said anxiously.

'Of course,' said Mma Ramotswe. 'Of course.'

They ate in silence, and contentment. The children, their mouths filled with syrup sandwiches, were quiet now, and again they could hear the birds.

'What we are trying to do with these children,' said Mma Potokwani suddenly, 'is to give them good things to remember. We want to make so many good memories for them that the bad ones are pushed into a corner and forgotten.'

'That is very good,' said Mma Ramotswe.

Mma Potokwani licked a small trace of syrup off a finger. 'Yes,' she said. 'And what about you, Mma Ramotswe? What are your favourite memories? Do you have any that are very special?'

Mma Ramotswe did not have to think about that. 'My Daddy,' she said. 'He was a good man, and I remember him. I remember walking with him along a road—I don't remember where it was—but I remember how we did not have to talk to one another, we just walked together, and were perfectly happy. And then . . . and then . . .'

'Yes?'

178

She was uncertain if she should tell Mma Potokwani about this, but she was her old friend, and she did. 'Then there's another memory. I remember Mr J.L.B. Matekoni asking me to marry him. One evening at Zebra Drive. He had just finished fixing my van and he asked me to marry him. It was almost dark, but not quite. You know that time of the evening? That is when he asked me.'

Mma Potokwani listened gravely to the confidence. She would reciprocate, she thought.

'Funny,' she said. 'I think it was the other way round with me. I asked my husband. In fact, it was definitely me. I was the one.'

Mma Ramotswe, recalling her discussion with Mma Makutsi, suppressed a smile. *That's two things I need to tell her*, she said to herself.

CHAPTER SIXTEEN

A Short Chapter about Tea

The tea regime at the No. 1 Ladies' Detective Agency was, by any standards, a liberal one. There was no official slot for the first cup of tea, but it was nonetheless almost always brewed at the same time, which suggested that it had a *de jure* slot in the day. This was at eight o'clock, when work had already been going on for half an hour or so—in theory at least—although Mma Ramotswe and Mma Makutsi often only arrived a few minutes before eight. The turning on of the kettle had become part of the ritual of opening the office for the day, alongside the moving of the client's chair away from the corner where it was placed at night and its positioning back into the middle of the floor, where it faced Mma Ramotswe's desk, ready for use. Then the window was opened the correct amount, and the doorstop put in such a position that it would allow for some circulation of air without admitting too much noise from the garage, a finely judged calculation which Mma Ramotswe herself undertook. After this there was a brief period for the exchange of information between Mma Ramotswe and Mma Makutsi—what Phuti Radiphuti had eaten for dinner the previous night, what Mr J.L.B. Matekoni had said about the bed he had dug for his beans, what Radio Botswana had announced on its early morning broadcasts, and so on. Once these snippets had been shared, the electric kettle would be boiling and the first, unofficial cup of tea would be served.

Official tea came two hours later, at ten o'clock. It was Mma Makutsi's responsibility to fill the kettle with water, which she did from the tap just outside the door that led to the garage. The sight of her holding the kettle under the tap was a signal to Mr Polopetsi that tea was about five minutes away, and he would then walk over to the sink on the other side of the workshop and begin to wash his hands free of grease. This, in turn, would be a signal to Mr J.L.B. Matekoni to reach a decision on whether he would carry on with whatever he was doing, and have tea later, or whether he was at a point in the mechanical operation to set his tools to one side and take a break.

Mma Makutsi made the tea in two pots. One was her own pot, rescued from disaster some time ago when one of the apprentices had used it as a receptacle for drained diesel oil; astonishingly, it was none the worse for that experience. That had been one of the more serious points of conflict between her and the two young men, and had resulted in an exchange of insults and a storming-out by Charlie. Now, as she poured the hot water into the tea-pots, she remembered that difficult occasion and wondered how Charlie was faring with his new business. It was undoubtedly quieter without him; there were none of the sudden shouts that used to emanate from the garage when something was dropped or when an engine proved recalcitrant. He had a tendency to shout at engines, using colourful insults, and although Mma Ramotswe had instructed him never to do this when she had a client in the office, the exclamations still came. And now all was silence; the young apprentice, whom Mma Makutsi had seen when she came into work, had a hang-dog expression on his face and seemed to be listless and unhappy. It would be no fun for him, she thought, now that Charlie had gone, and she wondered whether he, too, might hand in his notice to go off and do something else. That would inevitably provoke a crisis for Mr J.L.B. Matekoni, who would never be able to cope with just himself and Mr Polopetsi to do all the work.

Mma Makutsi filled her own tea-pot and then reached for the small tin caddy in which Mma Ramotswe kept her supplies of red bush tea. She opened it, looked in, and then shut it again.

'Mma Ramotswe.'

Mma Ramotswe looked up from her papers. She had received a letter from somebody who wanted

181

her to look for a missing person, but the writer of the letter had signed it indecipherably, omitted to give a proper address, and had not mentioned the name of the missing person. She held the letter up to the light in the vain hope of some clue, and sighed. This was not going to be an easy case.

'Mma Ramotswe,' said Mma Makutsi.

'Yes, Mma? Is the tea ready?'

Mma Makutsi held up the empty caddy and shook it demonstratively. 'We have run out of bush tea,' she announced. 'Empty.'

Mma Ramotswe put down the letter and glanced at her watch. It was shortly after ten o'clock. 'But this is ten o'clock tea,' she said. 'When we had tea earlier this morning, there was bush tea.'

'Yes, there was,' said Mma Makutsi. 'But that was the last bag. Now there is nothing left. The tin is quite empty. Look.'

She opened the caddy and tipped it up. Only a few flecks of tea, the detritus of long-vanished bags, floated down towards the ground.

Mma Ramotswe knew that this was just a minor inconvenience; fresh supplies of tea could easily be obtained, but this could not be done in time for morning tea—unless she left the office and drove to the supermarket. If only Mma Makutsi had told her earlier on that they were down to the last bag, then she could have done this before ten o'clock. She wondered if she should say something about this to Mma Makutsi, but decided that she would not. She was still concerned that Mma Makutsi might suddenly revisit her decision to resign, and an argument over tea was exactly the sort of issue to precipitate that.

'It is my fault,' said Mma Ramotswe. 'I should

have checked to see if we needed new tea. It is my fault, Mma.'

Mma Makutsi peered into the tin again. 'No,' she said. 'I think it is my fault, Mma. I should have pointed out to you earlier on that we were down to the last bag. That is where I failed.'

Mma Ramotswe made a placatory gesture with her hand. 'Oh no, Mma. Anybody can make that sort of mistake. One can be thinking of something else altogether and not notice that the tea is getting low. That has happened many times before.'

'Here?' asked Mma Makutsi. 'Are you saying that it has happened here? That I have forgotten many times before?'

'No,' said Mma Ramotswe hurriedly. 'Not you. I'm just saying that it has happened elsewhere. Everybody makes that sort of mistake. It is easily done. I cannot remember a single time when you have done this before. Not one single time.'

This seemed to satisfy Mma Makutsi. 'Good. But what are we going to do now? Will you have ordinary tea, Mma?'

Mma Ramotswe felt that she had no alternative. 'If there is no bush tea, then I cannot very well sit here and not drink any tea. It would be better to drink a cup of ordinary tea rather than to have no tea to drink.'

It was at this point that Mr Polopetsi came in. Greeting Mma Ramotswe and Mma Makutsi politely, he made his way to the tea-pot which Mma Makutsi had placed on top of the filing cabinet. He was about to reach for the pot to pour his tea but stopped. 'Only one tea-pot,' he said, looking at Mma Makutsi. 'Is this bush tea or ordinary tea?'

'Ordinary,' Mma Makutsi muttered.

He looked surprised. 'Where is the bush tea, Mma?'

Mma Makutsi, who had been looking away, turned and faced him. 'What is it to you, Rra? You drink ordinary tea, do you not? The pot is full of that. Go on, pour. There is plenty there.'

Mr Polopetsi, a mild man—even milder than Mr J.L.B. Matekoni—was not one to argue with Mma Makutsi. He said nothing as he picked up the pot and began to pour. Mma Ramotswe, though, had been watching.

'It's all right, Rra,' she said soothingly. 'Mma Makutsi did not mean to be rude. Unfortunately we have run out of bush tea. It is my fault. I should have seen this coming. It is not a big thing.'

Mr Polopetsi put down the tea-pot and picked up his mug, which he cupped with his hands, as if warming them. 'Perhaps we should have a system,' he said. 'When the number of tea-bags in the tin drops down to five, then it is time for us to get more tea. When I worked in the pharmacy, we had a stock control system like that. When there was only a certain number of boxes of a drug on the shelves, we would automatically order more.' He paused, and took a sip of his tea. 'It always worked.'

Mma Ramotswe listened in some discomfort. She glanced at Mma Makutsi, who had returned to her desk with her cup of tea and was tracing an imaginary pattern on her desk with a finger.

'Yes,' Mr Polopetsi went on. 'A system is a very good idea. Did they teach you about systems at the Botswana Secretarial College, Mma Makutsi?'

184

It was a moment of electric tension, thrilling in retrospect, but at the time it was dangerous to a degree. Mma Ramotswe hardly dared look at Mma Makutsi, but found her eyes drawn inexorably to the other side of the room, where the gaze of the two women met. Then Mma Ramotswe smiled, out of nervousness perhaps, but a smile nonetheless, and to her immense relief Mma Makutsi returned the smile. This was a moment of conspiracy between women, and it drew all the tension from the situation.

'We shall have to put you in charge of tea, then, Rra,' said Mma Makutsi evenly. 'Since you know all about systems.'

Mr Polopetsi, flustered, mumbled a non-committal reply and left the room.

'Well, that sorts that out,' said Mma Ramotswe.

CHAPTER SEVENTEEN

Photographic Evidence

On the morning that the No. 1 Ladies' Detective Agency ran out of bush tea, Mr J.L.B. Matekoni left Mr Polopetsi and the younger apprentice in charge of the garage. There was not a great deal of work—only two cars were in that morning, one, a straightforward family saloon, had been delivered for a regular service, which Mr Polopetsi was now quite capable of doing unaided, and the other required attention to a faulty fuel injection system. That was trickier, but was probably just within the competence of the apprentice, provided his work

185

could be checked later.

'I am going out to do some enquiries for Mma Ramotswe,' Mr J.L.B. Matekoni announced to Mr Polopetsi. 'You will be in charge now, Rra.'

Mr Polopetsi nodded. There was a certain envy on his part of the fact that Mr J.L.B. Matekoni had been given this assignment which should, in his view, have been given to him. He had been led to understand that he was principally an employee of the agency, an assistant detective or whatever it was, and that his garage duties would be secondary. Now it seemed that he was expected to be more of a mechanic than a detective. But he would not complain; he was grateful for the fact that he had been given a job, whatever it was, after he had found such difficulty in getting anything.

Mr J.L.B. Matekoni drove his truck to the chemist's shop where he had left the photographs for developing. The assistant there, a young man in a red tee-shirt, greeted him jauntily. 'Your photographs, Rra? They're ready. I did them myself. Money back if not satisfied!' He reached behind him into a small cardboard box and extracted a brightly coloured folder. 'Here they are.'

Mr J.L.B. Matekoni began to take a fifty-pula note from his wallet.

'I won't charge you the full cost,' the young man said. 'You only had two exposures on the roll of film. Is there something wrong with your camera?'

Mr J.L.B. Matekoni wondered what the other photograph was. 'Two photographs?'

'Yes. Here we are. Look. This one.' The young man opened the folder and took out two large glossy prints. 'That one is of a house. Down there,

186

round the corner. And this one here . . . this one is of a lady with a man. He must be her boyfriend, I think. That is all. The rest—blank. Nothing.'

Mr J.L.B. Matekoni glanced at the photograph of the house—it had come out very well and he could make out the figure of a woman standing on the verandah although the man on the steps, his head turned away from the camera and obscured by the low branch of a tree, could not be identified. But it was not Mr Botumile who was the object of interest here—it was the woman, and she was shown very clearly. He looked at the other photograph—it must have been on the roll of film already, taken some time ago and forgotten. He took it from the young man and stared at it.

Mma Ramotswe was standing in front of a tree somewhere. There were a couple of chairs behind her, in the shade, and there, standing next to Mma Ramotswe, was a man. The man was wearing a white shirt and a thin red tie. He had highly polished brown shoes and a gleaming buckle on his belt. And his arm was around Mma Ramotswe's waist.

For a few moments Mr J.L.B. Matekoni simply stared at the photograph. His thoughts were muddled. Who is this man? I do not know. Why is his arm around Mma Ramotswe? There can be only one reason. How long has she been seeing him? When has she been seeing him? The questions were jumbled and painful.

The young man was watching; he had guessed that the photograph of Mma Ramotswe was a shock. Some of the photographs he handled were like that, he was sure; but he did not normally hand them to the husband. 'This photograph of the house,' he said, pushing it into Mr J.L.B. Matekoni's hand. 'I know that place. It is off the Tlokweng Road, isn't it? It is the Baleseng house. I know those people. That's Mma Baleseng there. Mr Baleseng helped to teach soccer at the boys' club. He is good at soccer, that man. Did you ever play soccer, Rra?'

Mr J.L.B. Matekoni did not respond.

'Rra?' The young man's voice was solicitous. I'm right, he thought: that photograph has ended something for him.

Mr J.L.B. Matekoni looked up from the photograph. He seemed dazed, thought the young man; on the point of tears.

'I won't charge you, Rra,' said the young man, looking over his shoulder. 'When there are only one or two photographs on a roll, we don't charge. It seems a pity to make people pay for failure.'

Pay for failure. The words cut deep, each a little knife. I am paying for my failure as a husband, he thought. I have not been a good husband, and now this is my reward. I am losing Mma Ramotswe.

He turned away, only just remembering to thank the young man, and went back to his truck. It was so bright outside, with the winter sun beating down remorselessly, and the air thin and brittle, and everything in such clear relief. Under such light our human failures, our frailty, seemed so pitilessly illuminated. Here he was, a mechanic, not a man who was good with words, not a man of great substance, just an ordinary man, who had loved an exceptional woman and thought that he might be good enough for her; such a thought, when there were men with smooth words and sophisticated ways, men who knew how to charm women, to lure them away from the dull men who sought, so unrealistically, to possess them.

He slipped the ignition key into the truck. No, he said to himself; you are jumping to conclusions. You have no evidence of the unfaithfulness of Mma Ramotswe; all you have is a photograph, a single photograph. And everything you know about Mma Ramotswe and her character, everything you know of her loyalty and her honesty, suggests that these conclusions are simply unfair. It was inconceivable that Mma Ramotswe would have an affair; quite inconceivable, and he should not entertain even the merest suspicion along those lines.

He laughed out loud. He sat alone in his truck and laughed at his stupidity. He remembered what Dr Moffat had told him about his illness—how a person suffering from depression could get strange ideas—delusions—about what he had done, or what others were doing. Although he was better now, and was no longer required to take his pills, he had been warned that there could be a recurrence of such thinking, of irrational feelings, and he should be on the look-out for them. Perhaps that was what had happened—he had merely had a passing idea of that nature and had allowed it to flower. I must be rational, he told himself. I am married to a loyal, good woman, who would never take a lover, who would never let me down. I am safe; safe in the security of her affection.

And yet, and yet ... who was in that photograph?

*　　　*　　　*

With a supreme effort, Mr J.L.B. Matekoni put out of his mind all thoughts of that troubling photograph and concentrated on the photograph of Mma Baleseng and the house. He had been to see Mma Botumile at her own house, a large old bungalow just off Nyerere Drive. It was an expensive part of town, one in which the houses had been built shortly after Gaborone had been identified as the capital of the newly independent country of Botswana. The plots of land here were of a generous size, and the houses had the rambling comfort of the period, with their large rectangular rooms, and their wide eaves to keep the sun away from the windows. It was only later, when architects began to impose their ideas of clean-cut building lines, that windows had been left exposed to the sun, a bad mistake in a country like Botswana. In the Botumile house there was shade, and there were whirring fans, even now at the tail end of winter, and red-polished stone floors that were cool underfoot.

Mma Botumile received him on the verandah of the house, in a spot that looked out directly onto a spreading jacaranda tree and an area of crazy-paving. She did not rise to greet him as he was shown in by the maid, but continued with a telephone call that she was making. He looked up at the ceiling, and then studied the pot plants; averting his eyes from the rudeness of his hostess.

Eventually she finished with her call. 'Yes, Rra,' she said, tossing the cordless telephone down on a cushion beside her. 'You have some information for me.'

There was no greeting, no enquiry after his

health, but he was used to that now, and he did not let it upset him.

'I have carried out enquiries,' he said solemnly. He looked at the chair next to hers. 'May I sit down, Mma?'

She made a curt gesture. 'If you wish. Yes. Sit down and tell me what you have found out about this husband of mine.'

He lowered himself into the chair and took the photograph out of its envelope. 'I have followed your husband, Mma,' he began. 'I followed him from his work in the evening and I was able to establish that he has been seeing another woman.'

He watched her reaction to this disclosure. She was controlled, merely closing her eyes briefly for a few moments. Then she looked at him. 'Yes?'

'The lady is called Mma Baleseng, I believe, and she lives over at . . .'

There was a sudden intake of breath by Mma Botumile. 'Baleseng?'

'Yes,' he said. 'If you look at this photograph you will see her. That is her house. And that person there, whom you cannot see properly because of the tree, that is your husband going up the steps. Those are his legs.'

Mma Botumile peered at the photograph. 'That is her,' she hissed. 'That is her.'

'Do you know her?' asked Mr J.L.B. Matekoni.

Mma Botumile looked up from the photograph and addressed him with fury. 'Do I know her? You're asking me—do I know her?' She flung the photograph down on the table. 'Of course I know her. Her husband works with my husband. They do not like one another very much, but they are colleagues. And now she is carrying on with my

191

husband. Can you believe that, Rra?'

Mr J.L.B. Matekoni clasped his hands together. He wished that he had spoken to Mma Ramotswe about the proper way to convey information of this nature; was one expected to sympathise? Should one try to comfort the client? He thought that it would be difficult to comfort somebody like Mma Botumile, but wondered if he should perhaps try.

'I never thought that he would be carrying on with *her*,' Mma Botumile spat out. 'She's a very ugly woman, that one. Very ugly.'

Mr J.L.B. Matekoni wanted to say, *But she can't help that surely*, but he did not.

'Maybe . . .' he began, but did not finish. Mma Botumile had risen to her feet and was peering down the driveway.

'Oh yes,' she said. 'This is very well timed. This is my husband coming back now.'

Mr J.L.B. Matekoni began to stand up, but was pushed back into his seat by Mma Botumile. 'You stay,' she said. 'I might need you.'

'Are you going to . . .' he began to ask.

'Oh yes,' she said. 'I most certainly am going to. And he is going to have to too. I am going to ask him to explain himself, and I can just see his face! That will be a very amusing moment, Rra. I hope that you have a sense of humour so that you can enjoy it.'

As Mma Botumile left to meet her husband, Mr J.L.B. Matekoni sat in miserable isolation on the verandah. It occurred to him that Mma Botumile could hardly detain him against his will, that he could leave if he so desired, but then if he did that Mma Ramotswe would be bound to hear of his abandonment of the case and she would hardly be

192

impressed. No, he would have to stay and he would have to provide Mma Botumile with the support that she expected of him in the confrontation with her husband.

There were voices round the corner—Mma Botumile's voice and the voice of a man. Then she appeared, and behind her came the man whom he had heard. But it was not her husband; it was not Mr Botumile.

'This is my husband,' said Mma Botumile, pointing, rather rudely, to the man behind her.

Mr J.L.B. Matekoni looked from face to face.

'Well?' said Mma Botumile. 'Seen a ghost?'

Mr J.L.B. Matekoni was aware of the fact that Mr Botumile was looking at him in puzzlement and expectation. He decided, though, not to look at him, and concentrated on Mma Botumile instead.

'That is not the man,' he said.

'What do you mean?' asked Mma Botumile. She turned to her husband, and almost as an aside said, 'Your little affair. Finished. As of now.'

No actor could have dissembled more convincingly than Mr Botumile, were he dissembling, which Mr J.L.B. Matekoni rapidly concluded he was not. 'Me? Affair?'

'Yes,' snapped Mma Botumile.

'Oh . . . oh . . .' Mr Botumile stared at Mr J.L.B. Matekoni for support. 'It is not true, Rra. It is not true.'

Mr J.L.B. Matekoni drew in his breath. Mma Botumile, Mma Potokwani—these powerful women were all the same, and one just had to stand up to them. It was not easy, but it had to be done. 'He is not the man, Mma,' he said loudly.

'That is not the man I followed.'

'But you said . . .'

'Yes I said, but I am wrong. I saw another man leaving the office. He also drove a red car. I followed that man.'

Mr Botumile clapped his hands together. 'But that is Baleseng. He works with me. Baleseng is the financial controller. You followed Baleseng, Rra! Baleseng is having an affair!'

Mma Botumile directed a withering look at Mr J.L.B. Matekoni. 'You stupid, stupid, useless man,' she said. 'And that stupid photograph of yours. That is a picture of Baleseng going back to his wife! You stupid man!'

Mr J.L.B. Matekoni took the insult in silence. He looked down at the table, at the photograph, now revealed to be so innocent. A faithful man returns to his wife: that could be the title of that picture. He had made a mistake, yes, but it was a genuine mistake, a mistake of the sort that anybody, including this impossibly arrogant woman, might make. 'You're not to call me stupid,' he said quietly. 'I will not have that, Mma.'

She glared at him. 'Stupid,' she said. 'There. I have called you stupid, Rra.'

But Mr J.L.B. Matekoni was thinking. It now dawned on him that he did have some information that might be of use to these people, even if it was something of a long shot.

'I followed this Baleseng twice, you know,' he said. 'And on the first occasion I saw something very interesting.'

'Oh yes,' sneered Mma Botumile. 'You saw him go shopping perhaps? You saw him buy a pair of socks? Very interesting information, Rra!'

'You must not make fun of me,' said Mr J.L.B. Matekoni, his voice rising, but still just under control. 'You must not talk to me like that, Mma. You are very ill-mannered.' He paused. 'I saw him have a meeting with Charlie Gotso. And I overheard what they talked about.'

The effect of this information was dramatic. Mr Botumile, who had been quietly smirking ever since he had been cleared of suspicion, now became animated. 'Gotso?' he said. 'He met Gotso?'

'Yes,' said Mr J.L.B. Matekoni.

'What about?' asked Mma Botumile. 'What did they talk about?'

'Mining,' said Mr J.L.B. Matekoni.

Mr Botumile gave his wife a glance. 'We must hear about this.'

'Once you have apologised,' said Mr J.L.B. Matekoni, with dignity. 'Then I shall tell you about it. But not before.'

Mma Botumile's eyes widened. She was wrestling with conflicting emotions, it seemed, but eventually she turned to her husband. 'I'm sorry,' she said. 'We can talk later.'

Mr J.L.B. Matekoni cleared his throat. He had meant that she should apologise to him, and now she had apologised to *him*. She would have to apologise again, which would do her good, he thought, as this was a woman who had a lot of apologising to do.

As he waited for the apology, which eventually came, even if grudgingly given, Mr J.L.B. Matekoni thought: *I am a mechanic. I am not a detective. That has become well known.*

'Now, please tell us exactly what you heard them

talk about,' said Mr Botumile.

Mr J.L.B. Matekoni told them. There were holes in his account of what was said, but the Botumiles seemed ready to fill these in. At the end, smiling with satisfaction at what he had discovered, Mr Botumile explained to Mr J.L.B. Matekoni about share manipulation; about insider information; about having that precious advantage of advance knowledge. Charlie Gotso could have made a large profit on the company's shares, because he knew what was coming before anybody else did. And some of that profit, Mr Botumile explained, would go back to Baleseng.

'You've been an extremely good detective,' said Mr Botumile at last. 'You really have, Rra.'

'Oh,' said Mr J.L.B. Matekoni. He did not think that was true. Could one be good at something without knowing it? Could one accept the credit for an accidental result? Whatever the answers to these questions were, though, he had already made his decision. The things that we do best, he thought, are the things that we have always done best.

CHAPTER EIGHTEEN

We Deceive Ourselves, or are Deceived

'Now Mma Makutsi,' said Mma Ramotswe. 'I want you to tell me about your case. That small woman . . .'

'Teenie.'

Mma Ramotswe laughed. 'I suppose she doesn't

mind. But why do people put up with names like that? Sometimes we Batswana are not very kind in the names we give ourselves.'

Mma Makutsi agreed. There had been a boy in Bobonong whose name meant *the one with ears that stick out*. He had lived with this and had seemed unconcerned. It was also true; his ears did stick out, almost at right angles to his head. But why land a child with that? And then there was that man who worked in the supermarket whose name when translated from Setswana meant *large nose*. His nose was large, but there were people with much larger noses than his and it was only because of his name that Mma Makutsi felt her eyes drawn inexorably to that dominating feature. It was tactless and unkind.

'I don't think she minds being called that, Mma,' she said. 'And she is very small. She's also . . .' She trailed off. There was something indefinably sad about Teenie, with her pleading look. She wanted something, she felt, but she was unsure what it was. Love? Friendship? There was a loneliness about her, as there was about some people who just did not seem to belong, who fitted in—to an extent—but who never seemed quite at home.

'She is an unhappy one,' said Mma Ramotswe. 'I have seen that woman. I do not know her, but I have seen her.'

'Yes, she is unhappy,' said Mma Makutsi. 'But we cannot do anything about that, can we, Mma?'

Mma Ramotswe sighed. 'We cannot make all our clients happy, Mma. Sometimes, maybe. It depends on whether they want to know what we tell them. The truth is not always a happy thing, is it?'

Mma Makutsi picked up a pencil on her desk and idly started a sketch on a piece of paper. She found herself drawing a sky, a cloud, an emptiness, the umbrella shape of an acacia tree, a few strokes of the pencil against the white of the paper. Happiness. Why should she see these things when she thought of happiness?

'Are you happy, Mma Ramotswe?' Her pencil moved against the paper. A pot now, a cooking pot, and these were the flames, these wavy lines below. Cooking. A meal for Phuti Radiphuti, for the man who had given her that diamond, to show that he loved her, and who did; she knew that. A girl from Bobonong, with a diamond ring, and a man who had a furniture shop and a house. All that has come to me.

'I am very happy,' said Mma Ramotswe. 'I have a good husband. I have my house on Zebra Drive. Motholeli, Puso. I have this business. And all my friends, including you, Mma Makutsi. I am a very happy woman.'

'That is good.'

'And you, Mma. You are happy too?'

Mma Makutsi put down her pencil. She looked down at her shoes, the green shoes with sky-blue linings, and the shoes looked back at her. *Come on, Boss. Don't beat about the bush. Tell her.* She felt a momentary irritation that her shoes should speak to her like this, but she knew that they were right.

'I am happy,' she said. 'I am engaged to be married to Mr Phuti Radiphuti.'

'Who is a good man,' interjected Mma Ramotswe.

'Yes, who is a good man. And I have a good job.'

That was a relief to Mma Ramotswe, who

198

nodded enthusiastically.

'As an associate detective,' Mma Makutsi rapidly added.

Mma Ramotswe was quick to confirm this. 'Yes. An associate detective.'

'So I have everything I need in this life,' concluded Mma Makutsi. 'And I owe a lot of that to you, Mma. And I am thankful, really thankful.'

There was not much more to be said about happiness, and so the conversation reverted to the subject of Teenie and her difficulties. Mma Makutsi told Mma Ramotswe of her visit to the printing works and of her meeting with the people who worked there. 'I spoke to all of them,' she said. 'But they knew who I was—word got out very quickly after I had been identified. They all said that they did not know anything about things going missing. They all said that they could not imagine anybody stealing from the works. And that was it.' She paused. 'I'm not sure what to do now, Mma. There is one person whom Teenie suspects, and I must say that he seemed very shifty when I saw him.'

Mma Ramotswe was intrigued. 'Was that your instinct, Mma?'

'Oh yes,' Mma Makutsi replied. 'I know that you shouldn't judge by appearances. I know that. But . . .'

'Yes,' said Mma Ramotswe. 'But. And it's an important but. People tell you a lot from the way they look at you. They cannot help it.'

Mma Makutsi remembered the man in the office and the way he had looked away when she had been introduced to him. And when he raised his eyes and met her gaze, they darted away again. She would never trust a man who looked that way, she thought.

'Maybe he is the one,' said Mma Ramotswe. 'But what can we do? Set some sort of trap? We have done that before in these cases, haven't we? We have put something tempting out and then found it in the possession of the thief. You could do that.'

'Yes. Well . . .'

Then Mma Ramotswe remembered. Mma Potokwani had said something about this problem, had she not, on the picnic? There had been a child who was stealing from the food cupboard. And Mma Potokwani had solved the problem. Children, of course, were different, but not all that different when it came to fears and emotions.

'There is a story Mma Potokwani told me,' said Mma Ramotswe thoughtfully. 'She said that at the orphan farm they had a child who stole. And they solved the problem by giving the child the key to the cupboard. That stopped it.'

Mma Ramotswe had half-expected Mma Makutsi to reject the idea out of hand. But her assistant seemed interested. 'And that worked?' Mma Makutsi asked.

'No more thievery,' said Mma Ramotswe. 'The child had never known what it was like to be trusted. Once he was trusted, he rose to the challenge. Now, your shifty man at the printing works. What if he were put in charge of supplies? What if this Teenie person showed him that she trusted him?'

Mma Makutsi looked down at her shoes. *Give it a try, Boss!* She thought for a moment. 'Maybe, Mma,' she said. She sounded tentative at first, but then continued with growing conviction, 'Yes. I'll

200

suggest that he's put in charge of supplies. Then one of two things will happen: he'll stop thieving because he's trusted, or ... or he'll take everything. One of those things will happen.'

That was not the spirit of Mma Potokwani's story, thought Mma Ramotswe, but one had to acknowledge Mma Makutsi's realism. 'Yes,' said Mma Ramotswe. 'It will decide matters one way or the other.'

He'll steal the lot, Boss, whispered Mma Makutsi's shoes.

*　　　*　　　*

Charlie reappeared that afternoon. Mr J.L.B. Matekoni was involved with a gearbox and the younger apprentice was engaged in a routine draining of oil. Mr J.L.B. Matekoni, who saw him first, stood up and wiped his hands on a paper towel. Charlie, standing at the entrance to the garage workshop, made a half-hearted gesture of greeting with his right hand.

'It's me, Boss. It's me.'

Mr J.L.B. Matekoni chuckled. 'I've not forgotten who you are, Rra! You have come back to see us.' He looked behind Charlie, out onto the open ground in front of the garage. 'Where's the Mercedes-B ... ?' His voice died off at the end of the question. There was no Benz, and no car.

Charlie's demeanour gave everything away—in the way his eyes dropped, in the misery of his expression, in his utterly defeated posture. The younger apprentice, who had come over to stand next to Mr J.L.B. Matekoni, looked nervously at his employer. 'Charlie's back,' he said, and tried to smile. 'You see, Rra. He's come back now. You must give him his job back, Rra. You must. Please.' He tugged at Mr J.L.B. Matekoni's sleeve, leaving a smudge of grease on the cloth.

Mr J.L.B. Matekoni glanced at the grease marks. It was maddening. He had told these boys time and time again not to touch him with their greasy fingers, and they always did it, always, tapping him on the shoulder, grabbing his arm to show him something, ruining his overalls, which he always tried to keep as clean as possible. And now this foolish young man had left his fingerprints on him again, and this other, even more foolish young man had probably succeeded in destroying an old but perfectly serviceable Mercedes-Benz. What could one do? Where could one start?

He addressed Charlie, his voice low. 'What happened? Just tell me what happened. No this, no that. No, *It wasn't my fault, Rra*. Just what happened.'

Charlie shifted awkwardly from foot to foot. 'There was an accident. Two days ago.'

Mr J.L.B. Matekoni took a deep breath. 'And?'

Charlie shrugged. 'I could not even get it brought here,' he said. 'The police mechanic looked at it. He said . . .' He moved his hand in a gesture of helplessness.

'A write-off?' asked the younger apprentice.

Charlie moved a hand up to cover his mouth. From behind his fingers, his voice was muffled. 'Yes. He said that it would cost far more than it was worth to try to fix it. Yes, it's a write-off.'

Mr J.L.B. Matekoni looked up at the sky. He had brought these boys here, he had done his best, and everything they did, everything, went wrong.

He asked himself if he had been like this as a young man, as prone to disaster, as incapable of getting anything right. He had made mistakes, of course; there had been several false starts, but nothing ever approaching the level of incompetence that these young men so effortlessly achieved.

He felt a sudden urge to shout at Charlie, to seize him by the lapels of his jacket and shake him; to shake him until some sense came into that head of his, full, as it was, with thoughts of girls and flashy clothes and the like. It was tempting, almost overpoweringly so, but he did not. Mr J.L.B. Matekoni had never laid an angry hand on another and would not start now. The dangerous moment passed.

'I was wondering, Boss,' Charlie began. 'I was wondering if I could come back here.'

Mr J.L.B. Matekoni bit his lip. This was undoubtedly his chance to get rid of Charlie, if he wished to do so, but he realised, just as the possibility entered his head, that he was, in fact, relieved to have him back, even in these difficult circumstances. The car was still covered by his own insurance, but with the deductible element he would still be left out of pocket on its loss—almost to the tune of five thousand pula, he imagined. That was five thousand pula which Charlie's accident would cost him, and the young man would never have any means of paying that back. But these boys were part of the life of the garage. They were like demanding relatives, like drought, like bad debts—things that were always there, and to which one became accustomed.

He sighed. 'Very well. You may start again

tomorrow.'

The younger apprentice, overjoyed, seized Mr J.L.B. Matekoni by the arm and squeezed hard. 'Oh, Boss, you are such a kind man. You are so kind to Charlie.'

Mr J.L.B. Matekoni said nothing. He carefully extricated himself from the young man's grip and walked back into the workshop. There were more grease stains where the younger apprentice had held him. He could have fumed about those, but did not. What was the point? he thought. Some things just are.

He went into the office, where he found Mma Ramotswe dictating a letter to Mma Makutsi, who was writing it down in shorthand. He stood in the doorway for a moment, until Mma Ramotswe signalled that he should come in.

'It's nothing private,' she said. 'Just a letter to somebody who has not paid his bills.'

'Oh?' he said. 'And what do you say?'

'If you do not pay the outstanding bill by the end of next month, we shall be obliged . . .' She paused. 'That is as far as we got.'

'We shall be obliged to . . .' said Mma Ramotswe.

'Take action,' offered Mr J.L.B. Matekoni.

'Yes,' said Mma Ramotswe. 'That is what we shall do.' She laughed. 'Not that we ever take action. But there we are. As long as people think that you're going to do something, that's enough.'

'Bad debts are a very big problem,' said Mr J.L.B. Matekoni. He was about to add, 'just like bad apprentices' but he did not. Instead, with the air of one conveying very mundane news, he said, 'Charlie's back. Car crashed. Written off. He's coming back.'

Mr J.L.B. Matekoni was watching Mma Makutsi as he gave this news, and when he looked over in the direction of Mma Ramotswe, he saw that she too was looking at her assistant. He knew of Mma Makutsi's difficulties with the apprentices, and particularly with Charlie, and he imagined the impending return would not be well received. But Mma Makutsi, aware of their scrutiny, did not react sharply. There was a moment, perhaps, when the lenses of her large round glasses seemed to flash, but this was only because a movement of her head caused them to catch the light; not a sign. And when she did speak, it was quietly.

'That is a great pity for him,' she said. Then she added, 'So that is the end of the No. 1 Ladies' Taxi Service.' It was a simple epitaph, pronounced without any sense of triumph, without any suggestion of *I told you so*. As Mr J.L.B. Matekoni remarked to Mma Ramotswe over dinner that night it was a kind thing for Mma Makutsi to have said, worthy, he suggested, of top marks.

'Yes,' said Mma Ramotswe. 'Ninety-seven per cent. At least.'

They were seated alone at the table, Motholeli and Puso having eaten earlier and gone to their rooms to complete their homework.

'Poor boy,' said Mma Ramotswe. 'He was so looking forward to it all. But I'm afraid that I always thought it would end this way. Charlie is Charlie. He is the way he is, like the rest of us.'

Yes, thought Mr J.L.B. Matekoni; like the rest of us. I am a mechanic; that is what I am; I am not something else. I suppose I have my ways which annoy other people—my keeping those engine parts in the spare room, for instance—that annoys

Mma Ramotswe. And I do not always wash out the bath after I have used it; I try to remember, but sometimes I forget, or I am in a hurry. Things like that. But we all have some things we are ashamed of.

He looked at Mma Ramotswe. One of the things he was ashamed of was thinking that she could ever take up with another man, that she would leave him. He had tried to put those ideas out of his head because he knew that they were both unfounded and unfair. Mma Ramotswe would never deceive him—he knew that—and yet somewhere in the back of his mind those unsettling thoughts lurked, nagging, insistent. And then there had been that photograph. He had tried not to think about it, but he found that he just could not help it; try not to think of something and see how hard it is, he thought. There was Mma Ramotswe with another man, and the man had his arm about her. The camera had recorded it and he had found it. How could he *not* think about that?

Mma Ramotswe was buttering a piece of bread. She cut the bread into two pieces and popped one of them into her mouth. When she looked up from her task, she saw that Mr J.L.B. Matekoni was staring at her, with that look that he sometimes had, a slightly sad, confused look. She swallowed; a crumb tickled. 'Is there something wrong?' she asked.

He shook his head, in false denial, and turned away, embarrassed. 'No, nothing is wrong.' But then he thought, but there is something wrong. There is.

He closed his eyes. He had decided to say something because he could not keep this within him any longer. But he was unable to look at her while he spoke. 'Mma Ramotswe,' he said. 'Would you ever leave me?'

She had not anticipated anything like that. 'Leave you?' she asked incredulously. 'Leave you, Mr J.L.B. Matekoni?' And oddly, inconsequentially, she thought: leave you to go where? To Francistown? To Mochudi? Into the Kalahari?

He kept his eyes closed. 'Yes. For another man.'

He opened his eyes slightly, just to catch a glimpse of the effect of his words. What he had said surprised even himself, and he wondered what effect it would have on Mma Ramotswe.

'But of course not,' said Mma Ramotswe. 'I am your wife, Mr J.L.B. Matekoni. A wife does not leave her husband.' She paused. That was not true. Some wives had to leave their husbands, and she had done precisely that when she had broken up with her first husband, Note Mokoti. But that was different. 'Of course I would never leave you,' she went on. 'I have no interest in other men. None at all.'

Mr J.L.B. Matekoni opened his eyes. 'None?'

'No. Only you. You are the one. There is no man like you, Mr J.L.B. Matekoni. There is no man who is as good, as kind.' She stopped and reached out to take his hand. 'That is well known, by the way.'

He could not meet her gaze. He felt so ashamed of himself; but he was also touched by what she had said—for a man might easily imagine himself unloved—and he did not think it was untrue. But there was still that photograph.

He rose to his feet, gently pushing away her hand, and went across the room to pick up the small canvas bag which he sometimes took with him to the garage. He took out an envelope and felt within it for the photograph.

'There is this,' he said. 'There is this photograph. It was in the camera. That office camera.'

He pushed the photograph over the table towards her. Frowning, she picked it up and examined it. She looked puzzled at first—he was watching her expression closely, with anxiety, with dread—but then she smiled. Her smile struck him as callous, hurtful; that she should smile at, make light of such a thing as this. He felt doubly betrayed.

'I had forgotten about that,' she said. 'But now I remember. Mma Makutsi took it shortly after we had bought the camera. It was taken outside the shop where we bought it. You know that place, just outside the Mall. Look, there is that bit of wall at the back.'

He glanced at where she was pointing. 'And that man?'

'I have no idea who he was,' she said.

His voice was barely a whisper. 'You do not even know his name?'

'No. And I don't know hers either.'

'Whose?'

'Hers. The woman in the picture. The woman who looks like me. Or so Mma Makutsi told me. They ran that shop, you see, those two people. And Mma Makutsi whispered to me while we were buying the camera, *Look Mma, that lady is your double*. And I suppose she did look a bit like me, and when we mentioned it, they thought so too. They laughed, and so we decided to try the camera out. We took that photograph, and forgot about it.'

Mr J.L.B. Matekoni reached out and took the photograph. He peered at it. The woman looked like Mma Ramotswe, it was true; but on closer examination, of course it was not her. Of course not. The eyes were different; just different. He put down the photograph. He had been blind. Jealousy, or was it fear, had made him blind.

'You were worried,' she said. 'Oh, Mr J.L.B. Matekoni, I can understand now. You were worried!'

'Only a little bit,' said Mr J.L.B. Matekoni. 'But now I am not.'

Mma Ramotswe looked at the photograph again. 'It's interesting, isn't it,' she said. 'It's interesting how we can look at things and think we see something, when it really isn't there at all.'

'Our eyes deceive us,' said Mr J.L.B. Matekoni. He was feeling waves of relief, like that relief which follows a flood in a dry land after rains, sudden, complete, overwhelming; he felt that, but could not find the words for his emotions, and so he said again, 'Our eyes deceive us.'

'But our hearts do not,' said Mma Ramotswe.

A silence followed this remark. Mr J.L.B. Matekoni thought, simply, *yes*. But Mma Ramotswe thought: is that really so, or does it merely *sound* right?

CHAPTER NINETEEN

The Proper Place of Mercy

It seemed to Mma Ramotswe that a rather unusual, and unsettling, period had come to an end. If one believed those columns in magazines about the stars—and she had never understood how people could imagine that the stars had anything to do with our tiny, distant lives—then some heavenly bodies somewhere must have moved into a more favourable alignment. Perhaps the good planets had drifted from their normal position—which was directly above Botswana, and particularly above Zebra Drive, Gaborone, Botswana—and had now made their way back. For everything seemed to be in the process of satisfactory resolution. Mma Makutsi no longer spoke of resignation and seemed quite content with her new, vaguely defined post of as sociate detective; Charlie was back in the fold, the unfortunate No. 1 Ladies' Taxi Service no longer in existence, and, as a matter of tact, no longer mentioned, even by Mma Makutsi; Mr J.L.B. Matekoni seemed to have lost interest in conducting enquiries and had had his ridiculous anxieties laid to rest. Everything, in fact, seemed to have settled down; which was exactly the way Mma Ramotswe liked it to be. The world was full of uncertainty, and if the life of the No. 1 Ladies' Detective Agency and Tlokweng Road Speedy Motors, together with the lives of those associated with those two concerns, were all on an even keel, then at least some of that uncertainty was held at bay.

The world, Mma Ramotswe believed, was composed of big things and small things. The big things were written large, and one could not but be aware of them—wars, oppression, the familiar theft by the rich and the strong of those simple things that the poor needed, those scraps which would make their life more bearable; this happened, and could make even the reading of a newspaper an exercise in sorrow. There were all those unkindnesses, palpable, daily, so easily avoidable; but one could not think just of those, thought Mma Ramotswe, or one would spend one's time in tears—and the unkindnesses would continue. So the small things came into their own: small acts of helping others, if one could; small ways of making one's own life better: acts of love, acts of tea, acts of laughter. Clever people might laugh at such simplicity, but, she asked herself, what was their own solution?

Yet one had to be careful in thinking about such matters. It was easy to dream, but daily life, with its responsibilities and problems, was still there, and in Mma Ramotswe's case at least one pressing matter was still on her mind. This was her enquiry into the affairs of the hospital at Mochudi, and those three unexplained deaths. Or were they unexplained? It seemed to Mma Ramotswe that a perfectly credible explanation had been offered in each case. Ultimately we all died from heart failure, one way or another, even if there were all sorts of conditions which precipitated this. The hearts of these three had simply stopped because they could no longer breathe—or so claimed the

211

medical reports they had shown her. And if everybody knew why these three patients were finding it difficult to breathe, then surely that was the end of the matter? Did they know that? It was hard for Mma Ramotswe to decide, because the doctors, it seemed, could not agree. But then there would always be disputes by experts as to why one thing happened and another did not. Even mechanics did this, as Mr J.L.B. Matekoni had often demonstrated. He would shake his head over the work of other mechanics who had attended to cars before they were brought to him. How could anybody have thought that a particular problem was a transmission problem when it was so clearly to do with something quite different, some matter of rods and rings and all the other complicated bits and pieces which made up the innards of a car?

Mma Ramotswe felt helpless in the face of medical uncertainty. It was not for her to make a pronouncement about why somebody died, and if that was the case, as it undoubtedly was, then she felt that all that she could do here was to exclude, if possible, some non-medical factor, something unusual that had resulted in three people all becoming late at the same time of the week and in the same bed. It was for this reason that she decided that the only thing to do—indeed the final thing that she intended to do in this particular investigation—would be to go to the hospital on a Friday at ten o'clock, which was one hour before the incidents had taken place, and to find out if there was anything to be noticed. One would have thought that the hospital authorities, and in particular Tati Monyena, would have thought of doing something like this, but then it had often struck Mma Ramotswe that people who were in the middle of things just did not pick up what might be glaringly obvious to those outside. She often saw things which other people missed—a fact which rather bemused her; that is why I have found my calling, she said to herself; I am called to help other people because I am lucky enough to be able to *notice* things. Of course she knew where that particular ability came from—its roots were back in those early years under the tutelage of her cousin, who trained her to keep her eyes open, to notice all the little things that were happening when one did something as simple as go for a walk in the bush. Here, along the path, would be the tracks of the animals that had passed that way; there were the tiny prints of a duiker, the skittish miniature buck with its delicate miniature hooves; there were the signs of the labours of the dung beetle, pushing its trophy, so much bigger than itself, leaving those marks in the sand. And there, look, somebody had come this way while he was eating and had thrown the maize cob down on the ground, not all that long ago because the ants had not yet come to take possession of it. The cousin had an eye for these things, and the habit had been engrained in Mma Ramotswe's mind. At the age of ten, she had known by heart the number plate of virtually every car in Mochudi and had been able to say who had driven in the direction of Gaborone on any morning. 'You have eyes like mine,' said the cousin. 'And that is a good thing.'

Tati Monyena had responded enthusiastically to Mma Ramotswe's suggestion that she should visit the ward that Friday. 'Of course,' he said. 'Of course. That is a very good idea, Mma. I shall give you a white coat if I can find one which is . . .' He had stopped himself, but Mma Ramotswe knew what he had been going to say, but had not, was *if I can find one big enough*. She did not mind. It was a good thing, in her view, to be of her particular construction, even if the manufacturers of white hospital coats failed to make adequate provision for the needs of those of traditional build.

'That will be fine,' she responded quickly. 'I will not get in the way. I will just watch.'

'I shall tell the staff,' he said. 'You have my full authority. Full authority.'

He was there to greet her when she arrived. He had been watching from his window, she thought, which suggested to her a certain anxiety on his part. That was interesting, but not really significant. This whole issue was not one which a hospital administrator would like; it had required an unsettling enquiry, it made people uneasy; there were far more important things to do. And of course there was probably a personal factor, as there so often was. Mma Ramotswe had asked about and had discovered that the next promotion for Tati Monyena would be to that of Chief Administrator, a post which was already occupied by somebody else. But the woman who was in that post was also ambitious and there was a job in the Ministry of Health in Gaborone itself for which people thought she was the obvious candidate. That job was in the hands of a long-serving incumbent who was only eighteen months away from retirement and a return to a comfortable brick house he had built for himself in Otse. The last thing that Tati Monyena would want would be all these desirable changes to be disturbed by an

214

administrative hiccup, a scandal of some sort. So of course the poor man would be looking out of his window and waiting for the arrival of the woman who was to put this whole awkward matter to bed, whose word would be final. Nothing untoward, she would say in her report. The end.

He greeted Mma Ramotswe outside and led her to his office. She saw a white coat on the chair. 'For me?'

'Yes, Mma Ramotswe,' he said. 'It might be . . . it might be a slightly tight fit, I'm afraid. But it will mean that you will be unobtrusive. It's amazing how easy it is to wander about a hospital with a white coat on. Nobody will ask you what you're doing. You can do what you like.'

He said this with a smile as he handed the coat to her. As she slipped it on, though, his words lingered. *Nobody will ask you what you're doing. You can do what you like.* If, for any reason, there was a mischief-maker in the hospital, then the way would be wide open for such a person to do what he liked. The thought had a strangely chilling effect. It would take a particular sort of evil, she imagined, to prey on patients in a hospital; but such things happened—the unimaginable did occur. Fortunately she had never encountered it, but perhaps that innocence of experience would inevitably be shattered if one was a detective, which, after all, she claimed to be. But I'm not that sort of detective, she told herself; not *that* sort . . .

In her white coat, tight at the arms, she remembered how on another occasion, at the very beginning of her career, she had impersonated a nurse to deal with the bogus father of Happy Bapetsi. That had worked, and the greedy

215

imposter, who had claimed to be Happy's father, had been sent to Lobatse whence he had come, Mma Ramotswe's denunciations ringing in his ears. That had been a simple investigation, though, requiring no more than the wisdom of Solomon, and she had always had a clear idea of what she had to say, the lines she had to deliver. Her current circumstances were of course very different. She had no idea what she was going to say or do, or indeed of what she was looking for. She was searching for something unusual, something which had occurred at the same time on three Fridays, but she could not imagine what this might be. When she had asked the staff in the ward if anything special happened at that time of the morning, and on Fridays in particular, they had looked blank. 'We have our tea round about then,' one said. She had seized at this. Would nobody be looking after the patients while the nursing staff gossiped over a cup of tea? Her question had been anticipated. 'We take turns to have tea,' somebody else had quickly assured her. 'Always. Always. This means that there is always somebody on duty. Always. That is the rule.'

Tati Monyena walked with her to the ward, and introduced her again to the nurses she had already met. One smiled when she saw Mma Ramotswe in her white coat. Another looked at her in astonishment, and then frowned and turned away. They were busy, though, and had no time to speak to her. There was a man in a bed near the window who was breathing heavily, making a sound which was like that of gravel being walked upon. One of the nurses took his pulse and adjusted his pillow. There was a small framed photograph on the table beside him, left by a relative no doubt, a reminder, a little thing for a very ill person to have with him on his journey, along with all those other memories that make up the life of a man.

For the first little while, Mma Ramotswe felt like the intruder she was. It was an almost indecent feeling—that one was watching something that one should not be watching, like looking at another person in a moment of great privacy, but that feeling wore away as she stood by a window and watched the nurses at work. They were matter-of-fact in their manner: drugs were given, temperatures taken, entries made on charts. It was like an office, she thought, with its series of small tasks to be methodically carried out. That nurse over there, she thought, the one with the glasses, would be Mma Makutsi herself. And that young man who brought in the drugs trolley and who made some muttered comment to one of the nurses could be Charlie, and the drugs trolley, with its well-oiled, silent wheels, his Mercedes-Benz.

After three quarters of an hour, when she had begun to feel tired, Mma Ramotswe drew a chair over to the place where she had been standing. It was near a bed occupied by a silent, sleeping man. He had tubes inserted into his arms, and wires disappearing into the sleeve of his nightgown. He slept regardless, his face composed, peaceful, all pain, if he had been experiencing it, forgotten. She watched him and thought of her father, Obed Ramotswe, and of how he met his end, in just such a bed, and of how it had seemed to her at the time that a whole Botswana had died with him. But it had not. That fine country, with its good people, was still there; it was there in the face of this elderly man with his head upon that pillow and the sunlight, the warm, friendly sun of Africa, slanting through the window and falling upon him now in his last days.

She shifted in her chair and looked at her watch. It was almost eleven o'clock. The nurses, or some of them, would surely have their tea soon; but not today, perhaps, when they all seemed to be so busy. She closed her eyes for a moment, in comfortable drowsiness, feeling the sun from the window on her face. Eleven o'clock.

The double swing doors at the end of the ward were opened, and a woman in a light green working dress, the uniform of the hospital's support staff, bent down to put a doorstop in place. Behind her was a floor-polishing machine, a big, ungainly instrument like an over-sized vacuum cleaner. The woman glanced at Mma Ramotswe as she pushed her floor polisher in, and then she bent down and switched it on. There was a loud whining sound as the machine's circular pad rubbed at the sealed concrete of the floor, and a smell of polish too, from some automatic dispenser attached to the handle. This was a well-run hospital, thought Mma Ramotswe; and a well-run hospital would also be battling against dirt on floors. That was where the invisible enemies were, was it not?—the armies of germs waiting for their chance.

She watched the woman fondly. She was a traditionally built cleaning lady doing an important, but badly paid job. There was no doubt that a number of children would be dependent on that job, on the money that it brought for their food, their school clothes, their hopes for a future. And here was this solid, reliable woman doing her job, as women throughout Botswana would be doing their various jobs at that very moment; her floor polisher whirring, its long electrical cable trailing behind it and out of the door into the corridor.

She was Mma Ramotswe, and she noticed things. She noticed the length of the cable, and all its coils, and she wondered whether there were not places in the ward where the polisher might be plugged in. Surely that would be easier, and would mean that this long cable could not threaten to trip people up in the ward or in the corridor. That would be far more sensible.

She looked about her. The ward was full of plugs, one at the head of each bed. And into each of these plugs there were fitted the lights, the injection pumps, the appliances that helped the patients to breathe . . .

She rose to her feet. The cleaning woman had now almost drawn level with her and they had exchanged a friendly glance, followed by a smile. She approached the woman, who looked up from her work and raised an eyebrow in enquiry before she bent down and switched off the polisher.

'Dumela, Mma.'

The greeting was exchanged. Then Mma Ramotswe leaned forward and whispered to her urgently. 'I must talk to you, Mma. Please can we go outside and talk? I won't keep you for long.'

'What, now?' The woman had a soft, almost hoarse voice. 'Now? I am working now, Mma.'

'Mr Monyena,' said Mma Ramotswe, pointing in the direction of Tati Monyena's office. 'I am doing something for him. I am allowed to speak to anybody in working hours. You need not worry.'

The woman nodded. The mention of Tati Monyena's name had reassured her, and she pushed her polisher to one side and followed Mma Ramotswe out of the ward. They went outside, to sit on a bench beneath a tree. A goat had strayed into the hospital grounds and was nibbling at a patch of grass. It watched them for a few moments and then returned to its task of grazing. It was becoming hot again. The cleaner said, 'This is the end of winter.'

They sat down. 'Yes, winter is over now, Mma,' said Mma Ramotswe. Then she said, 'I noticed that you have a long cable on your polisher, Mma. It goes right out of the ward and into the corridor. Wouldn't it be easier to connect it to one of the plugs inside each ward?'

The cleaner picked up a twig from the ground at her feet and began to twist it. She was not nervous, though; that would have shown, and it did not.

'Oh yes,' she said. 'That's what I used to do. But then they told me not to. I was given very strict instructions. I should not use any of the plugs in the ward.'

Mma Ramotswe felt herself swaying. It was as if she was about to faint. She drew a deep breath, and the swaying feeling went away. Yes. Yes. Yes.

'Who told you, Mma?' she asked. It was a simple question, but she had to struggle to get it out.

'Mr Monyena himself,' said the cleaner. 'He told me. He called me into his office and went on and on about it. He said . . .' She paused.

'Yes? He said?'

'He said that I was not to talk about it. I'm sorry I forgot. I did tell him that I would not talk about it. I shouldn't be talking to you, Mma. But . . .'

'But I have his full authority,' said Mma Ramotswe.

'He is a kind man, Tati Monyena,' said the cleaner. And then, after thinking for a moment, she added, 'He is my cousin, you know.'

Which makes you mine, thought Mma Ramotswe.

*   *   *

She walked back to Tati Monyena's office, divested of her white coat, which she carried slung over her right arm. He was in, his door ajar, and he welcomed her warmly.

'It's lunch time,' he said breezily, rubbing his hands together. 'Well timed, Mma Ramotswe! We can have some lunch in the canteen. They do very good food, you know. Cheap, too.'

'I need to talk to you, Rra,' she said, putting the coat down on the chair before his desk.

He patted his stomach. 'We can talk over lunch, Mma.'

'Privately?'

He hesitated for a moment. 'Yes, if that is what you want. There is a special table at one end that we can use. Nobody will disturb us.'

They walked in silence to the canteen. Tati Monyena tried to make casual conversation, but Mma Ramotswe found herself too involved in her own thoughts to respond very much. She was trying to make sense of something, and the sense was not apparent. He knew, she thought; he knew. But if he knew, then why ask her? An outside whitewash—that was what he wanted.

They helped themselves at the hot food counter and made their way over to a small, red-topped

221

table at the far end of the canteen. Tati Monyena, sensing that something important was coming, had now become edgy. As he lowered his tray onto the table, Mma Ramotswe could not help but notice that there was a tremor in his hands. He is shaking because he senses that I know something, she thought. Now he is feeling dread. There will be no senior job for him now. This was not the part of her job that she liked: the painful spelling out of the truth, the exposure.

She looked down at her plate. There was a piece of beef on it, some mashed potatoes, and green peas. It was a good lunch.

Suddenly, without having thought about it beforehand, she felt impelled to say grace. 'Do you mind if I say grace for us?' she said quietly.

He gave his assent. 'That would be good,' he said. His voice sounded strained.

Mma Ramotswe lowered her head. The smell of the beef was in her nostrils; and that of the mashed potatoes too, a slightly chalky, earthy smell. 'We are grateful for this good food,' she said. 'And we are grateful for the work of this hospital, which is good work. And if there are things that go wrong in this place, then we remember that there is always mercy. As mercy is shown to all of us, so we can show it to our brothers and sisters.'

She did not really know why she said this, but she said it, and when she stopped, and was silent, Tati Monyena was silent too, so that she heard his breathing from across the table. 'That is all,' she said, and looked up.

When she saw his eyes, she did not need to tell him that she had found out what had happened.

'I saw you talking to the cleaner,' he said. 'From

my office. I saw you talking to her.'

Mma Ramotswe kept her gaze upon him. 'If you knew, Rra, all along, then why . . .'

He raised his fork, and then put it down again. It was as if he had been somehow defeated, and there was no point now in eating. 'I found out by chance, only by chance. I asked who had been present in the ward just before the third patient went and one of the nurses happened to mention that the cleaner had left the ward just before it happened. She always polished the floor there at the same time on a Friday morning. So I spoke to her and asked her to tell me exactly what she did in the ward.'

Mma Ramotswe encouraged him. She was keen to hear his description of events, and relieved to find out that it tallied with what the cleaner had told her. This meant that he was no longer lying.

'She told me,' Tati Monyena went on. 'She told me that she plugged her polisher in near the door. Near the bed by the window. I asked her how she did this and she said that she simply unplugged the plugs that were already in. Just for a few minutes, she said. Just for a few minutes.'

Mma Ramotswe looked down at her mashed potato. It was getting cold, and would become hard, but this was no time for such thoughts. 'And so she unplugged the ventilator,' she said. 'Just long enough for the patient to become late. And then she plugged it back in. But the damage had been done.'

'Yes,' said Tati Monyena, shaking his head with regret. 'That machine is not the most modern machine. It has an alarm, which probably sounded, but with the whirring sound of that old floor polisher nobody would hear it. Then when the

223

nurses checked, they found that the machine was still operating properly, but the patient was gone. It was too late.'

Mma Ramotswe reflected on this. 'So did the cleaner know what had happened?'

'She knew that there had been an incident in the ward,' Tati Monyena replied. 'But of course she did not know that it was anything to do with her. She . . .' He stopped. He was looking at Mma Ramotswe with an expression that said only one thing, *Please understand.*

She picked up her fork and dug it into the potatoes. A little skin had formed on the top, a powdery white skin. 'You didn't want her to know that she had killed somebody, Rra? Is that it?'

His voice was urgent as he replied; urgent, and full of relief that she should understand. 'Yes,' he said. 'Yes, Mma. Yes. She is a very good woman. She has small children and no husband. The husband is late. You'll know why. He was ill with that for a long time, Mma, a long time. She herself is on . . . on treatment. She is one of the best workers we have in the hospital, and you can ask anybody, anybody. They will all say the same.'

'It is not just because she is your cousin?'

This took him by surprise, and he looked aghast. 'That is true,' he said. 'But what I said about her is also true. I did not want her to suffer. I know how she would feel if she found out that she was responsible for somebody's death. How would you feel, Mma, if you knew that about yourself? And she would lose her job. It wouldn't be my decision, it would be the decision of somebody back there . . .' He gestured through the window, in the direction of Gaborone. 'Somebody in a big office

224

would say that she had been responsible for the deaths of three people and should be fired. They would say, carelessness. They wouldn't blame me, though, or the head of the medical staff, or anybody else; they would blame the person at the bottom, that lady. Fire the cleaner, and end the matter there.'

Mma Ramotswe took a mouthful of potato. It was slightly bitter in the mouth, but that was what truth was sometimes like too. She could think about this problem, and then think about it again, looking at it from every direction. Whichever way one thought of it, though, it would still have the same feel to it, would still raise the same questions. Three people had died. They were all elderly people, she had found out, and none of them had dependants. Nothing could be done to help them now, wherever they were. And, if they were anything like the elderly people of Mochudi whom she had known, people of Obed Ramotswe's generation, they would not be ones to want to make difficulties for the living. They would not want to see that woman put out of her job. They would not wish to add to her difficulties; that poor woman who was working so hard, with that other thing hanging over her head, that uncertain sentence.

'You made the right decision, Rra,' she said to Tati Monyena. 'Now let us eat our lunch and talk about other matters. Relatives, for example. They are always doing something new, aren't they?'

Now he knew what her grace had meant, and he wanted to say something about that, to thank her for her mercy, but he could not talk. He expressed his relief in tears, which he mopped at,

225

embarrassed, with a handkerchief that she supplied, wordlessly. There was no point in telling somebody not to cry, she had always thought; indeed there were times when you should do exactly the opposite, when you should urge people to cry, to start the healing that sometimes only tears can bring. But if there was a place for tears of relief, there might even be a place for tears of pride—for the people who worked in that hospital, who looked after others, who took risks themselves of infection, of disease—from an accidental cut, a needle injury incurred at work; there were many tears of pride to be shed for them, for their bravery. And one of them, she thought, was Dr Cronje.

*　　　*　　　*

The next day, Mma Ramotswe dictated a report for Tati Monyena's superiors, which Mma Makutsi took down in shorthand, ending each sentence with a flourish of her pencil, as if to express satisfaction at the outcome. She had told her assistant what had happened at the hospital, and Mma Makutsi had listened, open-mouthed. 'Such a simple explanation,' she said. 'And nobody thought of it until you did, Mma Ramotswe.'

'It was just something I saw,' said Mma Ramotswe. 'I did not do anything very special.'

'You are always very modest,' said Mma Makutsi. 'You never take any credit for these things. Never.'

Mma Ramotswe was embarrassed by praise, and so she suggested that they continue with the report, which ended with the conclusion that no further action was required in respect of incidents in which nobody was to blame.

'But is that true?' asked Mma Makutsi.

'Yes, it is true,' said Mma Ramotswe, adding, 'No blame can be laid at that woman's door. In fact, she deserves praise, not blame, for her work. She is a good worker.'

She looked at Mma Makutsi with a look that she rarely used, but which was unambiguously one which closed a matter entirely.

'Well,' said Mma Makutsi. 'I suppose you're right.'

'I am,' said Mma Ramotswe.

The report was finished, typed by Mma Makutsi—in an error-free performance, as one might expect of such a graduate of the Botswana Secretarial College. Then it was time for tea, as it so often was.

'You told that woman, Teenie, about the key to the supplies?' said Mma Ramotswe. 'I wonder how that went. It's a test of Mma Potokwani's advice, I suppose.'

Mma Makutsi laughed. 'Oh, Mma, I forgot to tell you. She telephoned me. She did as I suggested and put that man in charge of all the supplies. The next day, everything was gone. The whole lot. And he had gone too.'

Mma Ramotswe looked into her cup. She wanted to laugh, but prevented herself from doing so. This result was both a success and a failure. It was a success in that it demonstrated to the client beyond all doubt who the thief was; it was a failure in that it showed that trust does not always work. Perhaps trust had to be accompanied by a measure of common sense, and a hefty dose of realism about human nature. But that would need a lot of thinking about, and the tea break did not go on forever. 'Oh well,' she said. 'That settles that. Mma Potokwani's advice *sounded* good, though.'

Mma Makutsi agreed that it did, and they talked for a few minutes about the various affairs of the office until Mr J.L.B. Matekoni came in for his tea. He was wiping his hands on a cloth and smiling. He had been struggling with a particularly difficult gearbox and at long last he had solved the problem. Mma Ramotswe looked out of the window, at that square of land, at the acacia tree that fingered into the empty sky; a little slice of her country that she loved so much, Botswana, her place.

Mma Ramotswe smiled at Mr J.L.B. Matekoni. He was such a good man, such a kind man, and he was her husband.

'That engine I've been working on will run so sweetly,' he remarked as he poured his tea.

'Like life,' she said.